ENDING

Hilma Wolitzer

ENDING

1974

WILLIAM MORROW & COMPANY, INC., NEW YORK

Printed in the United States of America.

1   2   3   4   5   78   77   76   75   74

Design by Helen Roberts

Library of Congress Cataloging in Publication Data

Wolitzer, Hilma.
   Ending.

   I. Title.
PZ4.W8596En   [PS3573.O563]   813'.5'4   74-3473
ISBN 0-688-00304-4

To Morty, Nancy, and Meg

ENDING

1

I found myself lying in the middle of the bed on those strange new nights, like someone staking claim to territory in a wilderness. How was I supposed to sleep anyway? And I *had* to sleep, because it restored my body, if not my spirit, and because it was a dark and peaceful place to go. But I needed something, some ritual to work as a soporific. When Jay was there we had our own rituals, worked out over the years, and I missed them as an essential part of missing him. I suppose every married couple has something, a certain rhythm to the conversation, a settling of two bodies in the space of the bed. I imagined this happening everywhere, in apartments across the city, shoes dropping, droning synopses of the day's events. Complaints whispered, kisses, covers flung back, children calling out revelations in their sleep.

Jay and I always ended up the same way, our talk fading in final whispers: Are you asleep? Are you? Then one of his hands reaching above the pillows to hold the broad rail of the bed firmly, as if he were on a moving vehicle. It seemed there were always at least two perfect points of contact between us, sometimes foreheads and hands, or perhaps buttocks and soles of feet. Was it my need or his? I reached out now and found only the vast landscape of the bed, and myself alone in the quietest of nights.

I was used to sleeping alone when I was a child. But then the bed was narrow and chaste and not meant for confrontations. My parents' voices were on the other side of the wall like sounds heard through a drumskin. And I had rituals even then. Songs sung in a humming night-voice, lullabies that incorporated magic and kept me safe from the terrors I invented. Kept the shadows inanimate and peaceful, and the voices low and affectionate, or chose to drown them out altogether.

I tried my own voice out now in the bedroom. Hello? It sounded like a voice spoken in a furnished room. And there was no one to answer.

I needed something all right, something to relieve the lousy burden of consciousness. I thought if Jay could be there, even in my imagination, *that* would be the magic, the ritual that would give me peace. So I put him there in the room, his clothes falling in silent drifts everywhere, his bad habit. This room looks like a bomb hit it. Can't you ever pick up your own things? But in fantasy I held my tongue. I simply recreated his gestures, the clockwind-ing, those great stretches that brought his fingertips close to the ceiling. Then down at the foot of the bed for a few push-ups. Too tired, giving up. Good night honey, whis-pered through the floorboards to the mean old lady in the apartment under ours.

Then I moved to my own side of the bed and let my hand fall idly onto the cool empty space next to me. I remembered how Jay and I used to talk every night. It was the perfect time for the baring of feelings and the continuing exchange of histories. There was a sibling quality to us, the innocence of a brother and sister telling everything to one another. After all, we had each been that lonely creature, an only child. Used to the silences, that inward turn of the imagination, the inevitable bloom of fantasy. We confessed everything, giddy with the idea of a permanent companion at last, a night-friend, an answering voice.

I told about being afraid of shadows, dreading murder or worse in the ghostly form of monsters. "I slept with the light on until I was twelve," I told Jay.

"Poor sweetie." He stroked my face as if he were comforting the frightened child.

Encouraged, I told more, about singing into the basin mirror in a locked bathroom, imagining music behind me, enraptured audiences in front of me. I wanted to be a famous singer, even though I had a thin, timid voice. I didn't even really like singing that much, just the *idea* of it, the razzle-dazzle of lights, applause, fame. Something magical to bring my parents together, joined and proud in the front row, the way they were at rare moments such as school plays, graduations.

"What did you dream of the most when you were a kid?" I asked Jay.

"I don't know." He squinted as if he were trying to see, at the far side of the bedroom, the shadow, the afterimage of himself as a small boy. Then he remembered something. "Mostly just a feeling of power, I guess. Making myself into some kind of big shot. Building myself up every night, deflating again every morning."

"Then were you very unhappy?" Up on one elbow, almost hopeful, remembering my own bruised childhood.

But Jay shook his head. "No." He smiled. "Maybe I was

11

too dumb to be unhappy. I didn't know any better. I thought the Bronx was the world, my family the population. Listen, I remember that I loved the wallpaper in our living room."

"What, flowers?"

"Colonial figures, a man and a woman in white wigs bowing to each other all across the room. Gorgeous. Mismatched. In the corner he bowed to half his own behind."

"We had flowers, pink and silver."

"I thought my father was some kind of hero. He wore a hat. When he took it off there was a line across his forehead from the band. He left every morning and he came home again every night on the subway. He rose right up out of the earth under a sign that said, IRT. We'd walk home together and I carried his newspaper, like a dog."

"In your *mouth?*"

"Don't be cute, Sandy. We went upstairs and supper was ready. Jesus, I thought that lamb chops and mashed potatoes were the best possible food. And besides, I was madly in love with my mother."

I laughed.

"Don't laugh," he said. "It was serious. I figured on marrying her when I grew up. An endless supply of baby chops done the way I liked them, somebody to rub Vicks on my chest forever. She was the queen of my dreams. I never noticed she had fat legs until I was in high school."

"A regular little Alex Portnoy," I said, patting his cheek. "Boy, in your heart you must have really hated your father."

"Ah, how could anyone hate him? He was the last of the good guys. Louie. Everybody loved him. Some of Mona's cousins still talk about him as if he died yesterday. He used to push me on park swings until his arms fell off."

All that happiness, all that love, returned and doubled. It was impossible, and a mean pinch of envy urged me on. "But listen, kiddo, what were you going to *do* with him when you grew up and married his wife? Wouldn't it have been a little awkward?"

"I didn't work all the damn details out, Sandy. I guess I figured he'd stay on, like an old family friend or something. You know. The king is retired. Long live the king." And Jay's eyes seemed to grow darker with reflection or sorrow. What he regretted, I knew, was that his father had never known *him* as a man, the product of all that gentle paternity, those endless pushes on park swings. "I wish I had a decent picture of him," he once said, looking through Mona's old photograph album, where she had written in white ink on black pages. *Louie and me at Swan Lake, 1931. A pleasant day with Aunt Rose and Uncle Abe, May, 1936.*

I thought I understood his frustration, a man with all that expensive equipment—lenses, enlargers, filters, lights —who had only a brown, fading memory of his father, taken ages ago through the insensitive eye of a plain black box. And it bothered him too that he could not remember his father, the true essence of him, but only anecdotes enriched by fantasy, and small memories of what it was like to be a boy at thigh-level to a beloved man, memories of wing-tip shoes, hats, cigars, and of a short, vulnerable figure, receding in the distance.

But where was the *man?* As mysteriously gone as the boy himself, and the young woman who had been his mother, shading her eyes shyly for the camera.

I felt ashamed then for begrudging him a refined and better version of his memories. God, sibling rivalry! "Oh, I wish I had known you then!" I cried, really wishing it, crazy about my image of him. A small thin boy with dark

13

hair, waiting at the subway each night for the miraculous resurrection of his father. A boy who believed that veal cutlets came from wild animals called veals, who thought that babies were brought into the world through women's navels, who never, in early ecstacy, noticed his mother's fat legs.

We had worked so hard to convince one another of our infinite innocence, the dumb sweet quality of childhood that still clung to us and let us be forgiven for past and future sins. We were exhausted and we moved closer under the covers, touching hands. Jay's hand, with flat, blunt nails and long bones under warm flesh. His knees locked one of mine between them.

"Are you falling asleep?"

"Are you?"

Then his hand leaving mine, reaching up to the bed rail and holding on.

Later, during the night, I came half-awake to Jay making urgent motions against my back. "Sandy? Are you sleeping?"

I remember I thought, Oh, God, why does he have to get so horny in the middle of the night? I groaned, hugging the side of the bed, trying to restore my dream.

But Jay was sitting up. "Listen, you were right," he said. "I must have hated my father. Unconsciously. I must have wished him dead. I remember I was afraid he'd come back during the night, like a ghost."

"Oh Jay," I said, coming dizzily awake. "I was only kidding. You *loved* your father. Mona says you cried your-self to sleep for weeks. That you slept with his picture. All kids are afraid of ghosts that way."

"The subway," he said. "I still hate the goddam sub-way."

"Everybody hates the subway. I mean, what could you

possibly like about it? Getting mugged? The noise? *Fuck you* all over the walls? Jay, your father must have hated the subway himself."

"Yeah," he said. "I guess so." He sighed, sliding down again, reluctant to give up his guilt.

And I was the guiltmaker. A strange and terrible power. But I could heal too. I giveth and taketh away. "Go to sleep, will you? The baby will be up yapping in about five minutes."

"Yeah," he said again, dreamily, his voice receding in the darkness.

We came together again, and I thought sleepily, my husband, my brother, my friend. "Shh," I whispered to myself, to him. "Shh." I pulled the cover up, enclosing us. Hansel and Gretel asleep in the woods, under a blanket of leaves.

I was drowsy now, able to sleep at last. Even with a last thought of Jay, reduced to a strange boyishness in his hospital bed, virginal and dreaming, but with a truly scary future.

2

Jay was sitting up in bed, not sure what to make of himself in that room, or of me facing him from the visitor's chair, with my hands like nesting birds in my lap. A bar of sunlight slanted in across the foot of the bed, bypassing the cyclamen that wilted on the windowsill. Jay said, "Try and bring a few books. There's that thing on Churchill on my night table and see if you can get the new Pauline Kael. Don't forget the folder in the bottom left-hand drawer."

I said, "Do you need more pajamas? Do you want another pen?" And we went on like that for a while in sentences that might have been simple translations in a foreign language class. Are you hungry? Would you like the blinds closed? What time is it?, until my hands flew up restlessly to the sides of my face. I brought one hand down and looked at my watch.

"Do you have to go?" The question was so quick and

his voice so high with disappointment that I felt ashamed, as if I had been caught in a rude gesture.

"Yes," I said, "no, I could stay a while. The children . . ." My words trailed off. In this new setting, the green walls and the modest curtains, we had nothing to say to one another. On the first day we had disposed of all the obvious comments and the jokes about hospital odors, about the voice on the loudspeaker summoning doctors as if it announced sales in the bargain basement. Ladies, ladies, for the next hour only, on our lower level . . .

I stayed another half hour and then I left in a rush of activity when another patient was brought into the room to occupy the other bed. He was older than Jay and his wife walked behind him with her eyes down. "Excuse me, excuse me," he murmured, as if he had intruded upon us in our own bedroom.

Jay said, "I'll come with you to the elevator." He took my hand, now disguised in a glove, and we walked down the hallway. "Don't worry, sweetie—and drive carefully."

"I will. I'll bring the books."

"So long." His arm hooked across my shoulders, circling my neck. It was slightly painful, as if he were demonstrating strength and power that the sag of his pajamas and the shuffle of his bedroom slippers belied.

It had snowed lightly again and I wiped the windshield with my woolen glove until the sting of the cold came through to my hand. I put the radio on for company and part of the way home I listened to a song about eyes that haunted, like pools of night. "Like po-ols of night," I sang, "I ca-an't forget you."

Harry came to the door first. Even as my key turned in the lock, I could hear scuffling sounds on the other side. I bent to embrace him and he let me, his face passive.

How was it possible to be so controlled at five? Then his brother pushed between us and my face was wet with passionate kisses.

The baby-sitter, who is a neighbor's adolescent son, came from the living room with a cupcake in one hand and a radio pressed against his head as if it were a poultice to soothe an aching ear. There were crumbs clinging to his lips. The sight of him, that half-finished look, his shirt on his shoulders as if it hung from a wire hanger, filled me with sadness.

"Hello, Joseph," I said.

He tried out his voice. It was the strange croak of a large flightless bird destined for extinction. "Hello," he said. "How is Mr. Kaufman?"

"All right. Was everything okay here? Did you have any trouble?"

He shook his head and then Paul, my younger son, wrapped his arms around the tower of Joseph's legs. "Don't go home, don't go home," he begged with a false cry of love. A three-year-old's such a baby, still capable of innocent deceit. But Joseph believed him and was flattered.

I too wanted to cry "Don't go home!" as if that tall stooped creature with bitten nails, who was already loping toward the door, could save me from anything.

I went to see Jay every day, twice a day when I could manage it. When Joseph was unable to stay with the children, his mother would come. But this was less satisfactory, because his mother had an insatiable hunger for medical detail, for terrible truths. When she said "How is he?" there was a light in her eyes that pierced bone and traveled bloodstreams. Her arms folded under her breasts, she waited for answers that I couldn't give. But she would

18

know, even in the absence of words. Then, I thought, everyone in the building would know, as if a coded message were being sent in the clanking of the incinerator door and the moan of the elevator.

Every day Paul said, "Is my daddy in the hospital?" When I said, "Yes, you know. I told you this morning, I told you yesterday," he smiled.

Harry didn't ask. He knew where Jay was. He knew my moods with the sensitivity of a lover, but he gave no sign and no comfort. At night his head banged against the wall that separated our rooms. I wished then that Harry was my favorite, that I could love his mystery more than Paul's easy charm. Everyone loved Paul best; he hardly seemed to need me as well.

Jay said, "I feel better today. I know I feel better because I'm going crazy in this place."

The man in the other bed lay back with his arms folded behind his head as if he were taking a sunbath. Every time I looked at him, he was looking back and he was smiling.

I smiled at him too. I smiled at Jay, at the nurses, at orderlies who sang in the hallways with the easiness of people working in a summer field. Then I tried not to look at the other man at all. "Jay," I said. "I miss you."

He turned his head and slyly, out of the corner of his mouth, he whispered, " I miss you too. I'll come home and you can give me the golden cure."

"Oh, I will."

His hand moved carefully and came to rest in the slope between my knees. I looked at the other man. He smiled and looked toward the window.

"I really feel better," Jay said. But that night he stayed in bed when I walked to the elevator.

Joseph's mother was the baby-sitter. "Everything okay?"

she asked, and I looked away from that eager face, fat and flushed as if she had just bent over a hot oven.

Instead I cuddled the children, pulling Harry up onto my lap while Paul pushed to replace him. Then I opened my purse to pay her.

"They can do miracles today," she said cheerfully, and with the triumph of the last word, she waddled out the door.

3

My mother called on the telephone. "Come down to the shop," she said. "We'll give you a good wash and set. You'll feel like a million bucks."

"Ma, I don't need a wash and set."

"Come. Daddy will use a conditioner, a cream rinse."

I reasoned that maybe it would be good to look pretty for Jay, that my hair could be a disguise for the disheveled state of my spirit.

My mother and father have owned the beauty shop for so many years that it is as familiar as a room in which people live. The pink chairs are rooted to the floor in a tidy row, facing the long mirror like vain women. On the walls models showing the latest hairdos look down and smile with perfect teeth. The partnership in the shop was always more binding, more sacred than the marriage itself. There, pulling a comb through knots in customers' hair, my mother remembers old grievances: women, real and imagined, lies, truths more painful than lies.

My father, with an eye on himself in the mirror, pumped the pedal so that a customer ascended to his reach. He wore the latest style in jackets for hairdressers and a white ascot bloomed at his throat. The name *Mr. B.* was embroidered above the breast pocket. "Mr. B., am I dry?" called the women under the dryers.

My mother wore white nylon that revealed only shadows of her body underneath. Her name, Rose, was in red on the swell of her right breast.

All the sweet and bitter smells were still there, and the hum of the dryers and the dying and rising voice of WABC bringing the latest of the top one hundred songs in America. Most of the songs sounded alike in that drone of electrical equipment and no one really listened except once in a while when a particular song bleated through clearly and one of the women shouted, "Oh shh, quiet, it's *him!* Listen to that, it's my favorite song."

Then some of the other women would sing along, their eyes shut and their wet nails splayed in front of them.

"Sandy," my father said, coming to the door. "How's my baby?"

Oh, it was good to be that for a while, to be innocent with the plastic cape circling my body, to be led to the seat in the back where my father let warm water fall on my head like love. My mother came and went on rubber soles like a consulting physician during surgery.

My father massaged my scalp and he hummed something discordant with the music from the radio, and I thought of Jay. With my eyes shut, I saw the room that he was in and the blurred image of all the rooms I passed on the way to his, and the clinical business of death, the death textures of plastic and rubber and steel, of tubes

22

and wires. I sat up gasping, like someone just saved from drowning.

"Isn't that better?" my father asked, and he closed a warm towel over my ears.

4

I began to be jealous of Jay's relationship to the hospital. It was as if he had moved to a new neighborhood without me and had made friends I didn't know. He was familiar and easy with the terrain and the life-style, while I was a transient who came with clumsy packages of fruit and books and a restlessness to leave. It seemed to be some perversity on his part to be *there* when he could have been home, to be ill when he might just as easily have been well, to withhold the nature of his illness like some coy and precious secret.

One morning I met Dr. Block in the lobby of the hospital. He said that all of the tests had not been completed, that he had to have a total picture. But he was concerned. He looked at me sternly as if it were my fault that Jay had done so poorly on some tests.

"But, do you think . . . ?" I began.

"The tests are what count," he said sharply, and I was reminded of cold teachers who care nothing for classroom

24

performance. Jay would not be passed for his dear face, for a testimony from me or his mother or his children. Not for a petition signed by old friends in college, by aunts who still save letters he had written from camp. Not for old baby pictures, for his love of animals, his thin beauty, his watch ticking in my ear, for his dark hair, for the thumping of his love inside me. For nothing.

But I smiled at the doctor as if I might yet win him over. Then I went upstairs and Jay and I sat holding hands in the solarium.

"What I really need, kiddo," he said, "I can't get here."

"The cure."

"Don't even talk about it," he warned. "I'm dying."

I looked up, startled, but Jay was smiling at the union of our hands. "I'm dying for you," he said.

Across the room two elderly men in bathrobes played pinochle, slapping the cards against the table. Like Jay, they wore plastic identification bracelets, and I was reminded of banded birds.

"Last night," Jay said, "I woke up in the middle of the night. I was dreaming. I dreamed that I was in that old apartment in Brooklyn, with my father and Mona. Except that I wasn't a kid."

I felt a terrible dread. "I thought that you dreamed about me," I said.

"I do. You're in all of my *hot* dreams. Whatever I have, that's one of the symptoms."

"You've *always* had that," I said.

"But this was really strange. I was in my old bed. My father was alive. He was looking out through the window. My mother was cooking something. I wondered what I was doing there."

Later when we said good-bye at the elevator, Jay told me that the man in his room had gone home and that they had put a kid in with him. "I think it's something serious," he whispered.

Everyone has something serious, I thought. Then I remembered his mother. "Listen," I said. "Do you think I should mention all this to Mona, when I write to her?"

He looked thoughtful for a moment. Then he tugged absently on my hair. "No. Why should we get her worried over nothing? She's so far away and I'll be home before she'd even get the letter."

I nodded, happy to be in on the duplicity, on this light-hearted view of things. Then the elevator came, and like two people who are helplessly unable to end a long distance call, we said:

"Good-bye."

"Good-bye."

"I love you."

"Me too."

"Let the children call."

"Tonight."

"You'd better go."

"We're holding up the elevator."

"Call."

"I will."

"Don't forget."

"Good-bye."

"Good-bye."

During the night I woke up in the wide expanse of our bed and I wondered, What if it's true?

5

The boy in Jay's room had been reduced to an exquisite delicacy. His pallor, the drooping stalks of his wrists were like those of the saints in medieval paintings. I thought that if he were to take off his hospital gown we would find him transparent, and all of the intricate machinery pulsing inside him would be visible to the eye. He was a lovely boy. His name was Martin and when Jay introduced us, he pushed himself upright to shake hands with me.

Martin's hobby was photography and he couldn't believe his good luck to be rooming with a cameraman. He had been worried that he would be put into the children's ward with crying babies getting their tonsils yanked out. "This is terrific," he said.

"This boy knows something about lenses," Jay told me and Martin lay back against the pillows with a satisfied smile.

"Mr. Kaufman," he said. "One thing is I talk a lot. It's my bad habit. My mother says I'm like a phonograph.

When you want to, tell me to shut up. It's the only way to turn me off. I've always been like this, even as a kid. I drive my teachers crazy. Nobody can get a word in edgewise. So when you want to, tell me to shut up, and I will."

Jay told him that he was glad for the company, that he was lucky to have someone with the same interests in his room.

"Boy," Martin said. "What if I had some moody guy? You know, someone nervous. I'd drive him up the wall."

Martin seemed so sick that he made Jay appear well. It's only a trick, I thought, like something done with a camera. I looked at Jay sharply to detect any changes. Was he thinner, had his color changed? Did I ever mark all the subtle changes that had taken place since I first met him? When do we become mortal?

One day I walked into the room and something was being drained in through Martin's wrist from a bottle. "My shutter arm," he said in mock despair.

I brought an album of Jay's stills and they talked into the afternoon about openings and zooms, their voices rising and falling in a soporific wave: f.4.5, wide angle, f.11. We might have been a family in our own home on a winter day. But the secret fluid ticked into Martin's arm and the antiseptic stench was everywhere.

Martin's parents arrived. They were tall thin people who seemed too old to have a child of Martin's age. They both shook hands with us with a solemnity that might be reserved for formal occasions. The father had a hoarse rasp of a voice. The mother whispered, "Isn't this nice? I was worried that he might have been put in with someone" (here she paused and looked around cautiously), "someone very *ill*." She explained that Martin was recovering now, that he had been sick with terrible complications after his appendix had ruptured. "He's getting better now, but he was *desperately* ill." She was in love with the sounds of those words. *"Desperately,"* she said. *"Touch and go. In God's hands."* Was I to learn a new vocabulary? *"Life and death,"* said Martin's mother.

"That's right," his father concurred at intervals in his terrible voice.

"Martin is our only child," the mother said.

"That's right," said the father, as if we might not have believed her.

Jay and I decided to go to the solarium, another occasion for handshaking. Even as we walked down the hall, the chorus of their voices followed us: the main theme of the mother, the tired rasp of the father, and Martin, piping, clear, asking questions, talking, talking, hanging on.

At the elevator, Jay said, "I feel like a fool."

6

In the morning he called and said that the weather report was very bad, that the roads were slick already and that he didn't want me to come. He whispered because Martin was sleeping. "That poor kid," he said. "He was up all night."

I found myself whispering back. "If I stay home," I said, "maybe I'll bake something. Or I'll do hems. I'll write to your mother."

Jay said, "You don't have to do penance, Sandy. The roads are bad."

It was true. The matter was out of my hands. I didn't have to go. I *couldn't* go. I looked out through the window for reassurance and saw the whiteness and felt the windowpane shudder with the thrust of the wind.

"Is my daddy in the hospital?" Paul asked, peering into the depths of his soup.

"You know perfectly well," I said.

"Perfectly well," he echoed. "Perfectly well."

Harry was drawing a picture for Jay. It was a scene of a summer's day with V-shaped birds in flight across a blazing sky, and oval clouds, and in the corner a very small figure launching a kite.

"Daddy will love it," I told him. "That's a wonderful picture. He'll show it to everybody," I said. "He'll really love it." When I went to see Jay again, I would put Harry's picture on the nightstand next to the cards from friends and the plant from the camera crew. Everyone had sent get-well cards, the sort that ridicule any indulgence in sickness, that threaten you to get well quickly (or else!), that make wisecracks about expensive doctors and sexy nurses.

In the afternoon I didn't bake or sew or even write to Jay's mother. I called my friend Isabel on the telephone.

"Are you scared?" she asked.

"Yes."

"I don't know what to say, Sandy. I want to say maybe it will be all right. But I'm afraid you might hate me for it."

"I wouldn't, Izzy."

"You might. False hopes are cruel, because they make you seem less than you are. Remember when everyone used to say that Eddie would come back, that it was only a fling?"

"Yes."

"I wanted to believe them, but I despised them at the same time for fooling me. I wanted to believe anything. I loved stories about other people: distant cousins, old neighbors who had been through it all and survived. Men who came back with their tails between their legs. Wives who were celebrated with ticker-tape parades and monuments to their righteousness. But it is different for you, Sandy. There's hope. I mean you don't know yet."

"That's right. Mrs. L., Joseph's mother, knows hundreds of *identical* cases. They were all saved by Alka-Seltzer or something."

"How does he feel?"

"Mostly tired. He *wakes up* tired. He looks lousy and his back aches."

"Do you want to come here? Do you want to stay with me?"

I thought about Isabel's apartment, of the four places set at the table for the three children and herself, the displacement of male character in every room. Like a liquid, she had spilled over onto all the places Eddie had been. Her papers and books were scattered on his old desk, her makeup in crazy disorder everywhere. Her belongings swelled in closets and drawers.

"Thanks," I said. "We're okay."

Later I sat on the sofa and watched television, while Harry and Paul pushed toy cars across the floor and through the tunnel between my feet. I watched quiz programs and a woman from Ohio won two cars. She screamed, she wept, she banged her hands on the podium. "I never won anything in my life!" she cried. Tears came to my own eyes. The cars revolved slowly on a turntable and the woman applauded as if they were performers. Her husband ran up onto the stage from the audience and kissed her feverishly.

I watched an old movie with a shaky sound track and a happy ending and the tears kept rolling down my cheeks. I snuffled and wiped them away with the back of my hand. Harry fell asleep with his hand across one of his toys and Paul climbed up into my lap and sucked his thumb with greedy pleasure. I watched two soap operas. In the second one, the scene opened in a hospital corridor and an orderly was wheeling a stretcher from the operating theater. There was a child on the stretcher. The child's head was swathed in bandages. A young couple rushed from off-camera to the child's side.

"Not now, Mrs. Burns, not now," said a voice, and they looked up imploringly at the face of the surgeon. "It's going to be all right," he said, and the camera panned to his beautiful scrubbed hands as he stroked the cheek of the unconscious child.

"Thank God!" bawled Mrs. Burns. "Oh oh thank God!" She wept into her white gloves.

"Thank *you,* Dr. Peters," said Mr. Burns.

Organ music swelled inside my breast. My throat was thick with tears.

I watched a situation comedy with canned laughter, about a mix-up in party invitations. Someone fell over a kid's bicycle and down a flight of stairs. Someone brought a monkey dressed as a little girl into the house. The laughter went on and on and I couldn't stop crying. Even when Paul looked up and said, "Don't!" Even when I smiled and made laughing noises and pointed at the screen. "Look at the s-silly monkey," I sobbed. "Oh God, look at the f-funny m-m-monkey. Oh ha ha oh God," gasping and gagging until the commercial when I blew my nose and began to grow calm again.

The next day there was a letter from Jay's mother. She lives in Hawaii with her second husband. They are semiretired now, working part time in a plant that packages tiny orchids in plastic vials and then ships them to California for distribution at the openings of gas stations and supermarkets. They've lived there for six months and so far she has sent a grass skirt for me, toy ukeleles for the children and a record with instruction book, called *The Beautiful Language of Hula Hands.*

January 5th

Dear Children,

Aloha! How are you? Fine I hope. We are fine living the life of Riley and enjoying ourselves. You can't imagine the interesting people we are meeting from all walks of life. Sam says what difference does it make what you are if you are a good person in your heart. You know him he is soft.

Seventy nine degrees here today can you believe it I am wearing only a sleeveless cotton dress in January. Please look out for a package I am sending for the children how are they? Fine I hope. Give them a big kiss. Sam says Aloha too. He is becoming an artiste in his old age and does nice paintings of the scenery. We will send you a good one to hang up. There are some girls here with bathing suits like diapers. Sam says he will come back here in the next life. You would not recognize us we are black.

Love,
Mona

7

I have early sensuous memories of my father: the scratch of his moustache when he feasted at my throat, the exotic scent of the beauty shop that clung to his clothing and his skin, the resonance of his voice and the resultant joy in my chest at the sound of it. There was also the stern glance of my mother, frowning on frivolity.

Did I imagine their quarrels on the other side of the wall? How does a child learn such things? My mother made no mystery of them. There is a language specifically for that sort of quarrel. And I observed my father in the shop, touching the women as he spoke to them, his hand on someone's shoulder, his fingers stroking pleasure into another's scalp. I sat on a chair spinning around and around, catching myself in the mirrors everywhere, in love with my blond hair, with my own known face.

I imagined then that my father's affairs were those of the heart, in the romantic sense induced by movies I had seen and magazines I had read after school in the beauty shop. In my mind he did harmless things, necessary to his sentimental spirit. I believed that he clinked wine glasses with pretty women, and danced intricate tango steps and laughed a great deal over innocent jokes.

But the language on the other side of the wall was more specific. "Tramp." "Bum." "Whore."

Yet they were serious business partners. When they checked the day's receipts, when they studied the hair-dye charts or the inventory on shampoos and rinses, there was a harmony and order that never existed in their other life.

One night, shortly after we were married, Jay and I were lying in bed together. We had come from a party an hour before and we floated in that limbo between wakefulness and sleep. I don't remember the series of thoughts that brought me back to those former nights, but I was there again, lying in that white narrow bed, in a room that harbored different dreams. I heard the routine noises again: the dropping of a shoe with a weary thud, the sliding of drawers, the rise of my mother's voice, my father's answer extended into a yawn. The restless creak of bedsprings, another shoe. I was home in my own bed, lulled by the anesthetic of familiar sounds.

But then I was awakened by new sounds, the ones that threatened and alarmed: my mother's voice rising, rising, the hard, flat counterpoint of my father's. He told her that she was crazy, that she had a wild imagination.

"You're crazy," she said. "You're the one who's crazy if you think I'll stand for it. One whore after another. Do you think I'm stupid?"

He told her that she was cold, that she punished him for what existed only in her mind.

She warned that he did not know what punishment **was**, that she would show him, that she would teach him.

But two days later, no more, I came from school **and** found him leaning back in a shampoo chair, with his eyes shut. My mother was bending over him like a lover, washing his hair.

The memory made me wakeful and I sat up next to Jay in the bed. I began to talk about my parents and the pattern of their life together.

"She never forgave him," Jay said.

"No."

"Did you?"

"*Me?* He wasn't unfaithful to *me.*"

"In a way," Jay said, "all fathers are unfaithful to their daughters."

"I felt sorry for him. I don't know why."

"For him?"

"Oh, for her too. She worked so hard. She always looked so disappointed, so bitter. But my father had an air of innocence that seemed to absolve him. He was like a naughty but appealing boy. Everyone always liked him more than they liked my mother."

"But he wasn't innocent."

I sighed. "Not in the real sense of the word. Listen, he still has an eye for the girls."

"And your mother still has her eye on him."

"Yes."

Jay stroked the back of my neck with one finger. "Would you let me off that easily?" he asked.

"You?"

"Yeah, under the same circumstances."

"The circumstances couldn't be the same. You're not like my father . . ."

"But would you let me off?"

"I suppose I would kill you."

Jay laughed. "How?"

"How? I don't know. I guess I'd hack you up. An ax murder."

"Which part first?"

"Ha ha."

"I wouldn't let you off either," Jay said.

"What would you do?"

"Don't find out," he said. His hands moved under the covers.

"Is that what you'd do?"

"Maybe. Or this, or this."

"Chop chop," I said, reaching for him. He shuddered and I laughed.

"Shhh," Jay said. "Don't." Then the play stopped and we became serious. We touched each other slowly, deliberately, armed with new ideas and a strange new excitement.

8

Martin was sitting up in bed and crying. He rubbed his fist against his eyes. "I'm very emotional, Mrs. Kaufman. I can't help it. I know it's only tests, but I got scared anyway, when I saw him."

But Jay *was* frightening, lying there in sleep, back from a treacherous journey, looking smaller, more wasted than he had before. His mouth was open, his brow wrinkled as if in deep thought, and a gentle snoring sound came with each breath.

I said, "Martin, that's nothing to be ashamed of."

"Even in the movies or a book I feel terrible when something happens to somebody. I get involved with the characters until I get emotional. Some characters I feel like I've known all my life."

"The authors would be crazy about you," I said. "Listen, if you don't get involved you don't feel anything at all. That would be worse."

He looked at Jay again. "I thought it was something

terrible. I acted like a baby. I'll be surprised if they don't move me down to the kids' ward."

"Jay wouldn't let them. He *needs* you here," I told him.

"He was talking out of his mind," Martin said.

My heart seemed to fall sideways in my chest. "What did he say?"

"A lot of stuff." He hesitated. "A lot of crazy stuff. Once he said, 'I don't want to,' as if he was arguing with somebody. And some curse words. He didn't even know he was saying them." Martin flushed.

I sat in the chair next to Jay's bed without touching him. I sat there for two hours but he didn't wake up so I blew a kiss to Martin, who waved at me, and then I tiptoed out of the room.

9

Dr. Block had a bad cold. In fact, his nurse confided, he had come to the hospital specifically to see me. This news so rocked my being that I had to touch the wall for balance on the way to his consultation room.

He blew his nose with a noise of geese honking and he motioned me into the chair facing him. There we sat for a few moments, each studying the other's face. I sighed then, a signal that I was ready, and he began. "Mrs. Kaufman, I'm very, very sorry," he said, and I held up my hand to ward off his news, to bring the onrush of traffic to an instantaneous halt. But he continued, his running nose and eyes giving the illusion of weeping, his voice a monotonous counterpoint to his words. "I can't make it easier," he said. "I don't know how. It's in his very bones. In the marrow," He waited. Then, "It's called multiple myeloma. Tumors in the marrow, actually."

Marrow, marrow, I thought wildly of soup bones.

He paused, waiting for me to speak, to ask questions

and lead him into answers. But I was struck dumb and he began again, like an actor picking up the cues for some poor cluck mute with stage fright. "He's not in much pain. He may not be." His voice rushed through the tunnel of wind in my ears. "There aren't remissions with this, usually. We'll give him medication, and we'll keep him as comfortable as we can. But he will grow weaker. It will probably be a matter of weeks, maybe months."

I stared at him as if the words themselves were visible as they left his mouth, rising over his head and dissolving in a vapor. Was he thinking then of going home, to hot tea and lemon, of *his* wife pulling off her slip at bedside in a white pool of lamplight? Why didn't he call me by my first name if he wanted me to believe those terrible lies he told me about my husband, about his poor invaded bones, his failure to do well on tests, his irrevocable doom? Then my voice came up through my throat like rusty water forced through unused plumbing. "And Jay?" I asked. "What about Jay?"

Dr. Block knew what I meant. He stroked his jaw, was thoughtful. "No, I wouldn't tell him," he said finally. "Not yet, I think. Because"—he rummaged in his bag of words— "because then you remove hope."

Hope! The word was senseless, a stupid, blunt dud of a word.

"Of course," he said, "we don't know everything. There *is* always some element of hope. There is research . . ." I raised my hand. He touched it in midair and it fell to the desk between us.

In the parking lot, two women with linked arms walked cautiously across the ice to their car. "Be careful or we'll break our necks," one said.

"Just what I need," said the other.

It was a clear night, the roofs of the cars frosted in artificial light. I looked back at the hospital, where only shadows moved behind the yellow blocks. The motor of the women's car gunned in the silence and then they were gone. I walked to my own car, surprised that I remembered where it was parked.

In the distance a dog barked a high yipping complaint and I thought that dogs have no foreknowledge of death. If Jay had been a dog he would die anyway, but without dread and without longing. Jay loved dogs, had always wanted one, but they don't allow animals in our apartment building. The life-span of a dog is very short. Do dogs mourn for dead people? Our children had turtles kept in a glass bowl with a plastic palm tree on a center island. Harry would let them walk up the soft flesh of his inner arm. I will never to the end of my life know what Harry is feeling. Is there something wrong with Harry that I cannot know what he's feeling or thinking? Is there something wrong with me?

I didn't want to go home or anywhere else. What if I had not come at the doctor's summons? Would that have kept Jay's sentence suspended in time? I leaned against the hood of the car like a suspect waiting to be frisked. I believed then that I was crazy. I thought that I was capable of any act: laughing as easily as howling, dancing, stealing a car, shooting off a gun, lighting fires, driving with my eyes shut, anything.

If I was not crazy, why didn't I simply think of Jay? Why didn't I review love and happiness or weep for real loss, forever and forever and forever? I leaned against the car, dry and panting as an animal pursued and cornered.

A man asked, "Are you having any trouble? Is your lock frozen?"

I didn't have a voice yet. His shadow fell across my face. "Are you all right?"

"Yes," I said. "Ha. Maybe I'm crazy. Do I look crazy?"

He removed my hands from the hood of the car and made me face him. "Can you walk?" He led me across the parking field to a blue station wagon. He took keys from his pocket and opened the door. I was shivering now and my teeth were jumping in my head. He moved a baby's car seat from the front and then he guided me in.

"Listen," I told him. "Jay is dying."

"Your kid? Your husband?"

"Yes. I've known him since *high* school. High-school sweethearts. Nobody else." My body jerked in little spasms.

"Oh Jesus," he said. He leaned across me and unlocked the glove compartment. He took a small silver flask out, opened it and held it to my mouth. The whiskey was swallowed fire. "What's your name?" he asked.

"Sandy," I answered, reduced to only one name.

"Okay, Sandy. My name is Francis—Frank. Sandy? Listen to me. You're not crazy. It's a terrible thing that you're suffering, that you're going to suffer. Nobody can say anything or do anything to make it different or make it easier. Are you listening to me, Sandy?"

I only nodded and he took my hand and held it in the palm of his. "Do you have children?" he asked.

I held my other hand up in a V-sign. "Two."

"Ah," he said. "Do you want another drink?"

"No." I sighed, caught my breath, giggled.

Francis smiled and squeezed my hand. "You don't look like a boozer. You look like a nice girl."

"I used to be."

"What do you mean, *used* to be?"

"Now I don't know what I am, what I'm going to do."

"You'll do all right. I'm a good judge."

44

"I thought I would do something crazy."

"Not you," he said. "Do you want to talk about it—about Jay?"

"I can't. I can't even concentrate."

"Will you promise to go home then and get into bed? Can you drive?"

"Yes," I said. "I can't tell you . . ."

"Don't." He turned the key in the ignition. "Don't tell me." We drove in silence to the other side of the parking lot and my car. Francis took my keys and opened the door for me. He leaned over and kissed me on the forehead. "I'm not worried about you, Sandy," he said, and he waited with his headlights shining like beacons until my car curved out of the parking lot and onto the road.

Harry has always been a thin child, his bones sharp and urgent when you put your arms around him. One of the things he does is refuse to eat. My mother says that he is wasting away to nothing and she pokes tidbits at the unyielding slit of his mouth. She cajoles and wheedles. "Harry loves Grandma's hamburger patties. Harry only wants *Grandma's* vegetable soup."

But who knows what Harry wants? He is not wasting away, he is growing. He is incalculably strong, his fists hard knots on the ends of those thin arms.

Yet I could not resist the game either. I plied him with *my* specialities, seduced him with rice and chicken and eggs.

Jay said, "Leave him alone. He'll come around."

I knew that he was right and for a long time I placed things before Harry and stepped back like a mute but anxious servant.

Then one day, in a rage that entered me like a blade, I shouted, "Eat, eat, damn you! Eat, eat, eat," shaking his shoulders until his head wobbled in a blur before me and I was spent.

Coming home from the hospital, I wondered about Harry and about me as if we were star-crossed lovers. What was happening to Jay made all of us seem so fragile. Old guilts stepped up like children in a school play to recite themselves. How could I have shaken such a small child? What happens to love? And if Jay was dying (dying!), why had I not been better, as well, with him?

Joseph was there, pale in the light and shadows of the television set. I willed it and he didn't ask me anything.

The boys were asleep. I walked from room to room as if I were assessing the value of our lives. Jay had asked me to bring him two of his cameras. I set them aside on the dresser in our bedroom and then I went back and took one of them from its case. I walked around with the camera, peering through the viewfinder, seeing everything a frame at a time. I wondered why we choose to live out our lives in rooms like these. I looked at lamps and ashtrays and tables and chairs. I went into the kitchen and looked at two bananas on the counter, at the clock above the sink, at a gray scratch on the wall where Jay's chair scraped when he pushed it away from the dinner table.

Then I went to the window and saw my encapsulated view of Rego Park, the high-rise buildings like guardians of the lit and empty playgrounds. Did I want to live here? Did it matter? A few people, foreshortened and looking furtive, hurried into buildings. In the distance cars rumbled on Queens Boulevard.

I put the camera back into its case and went into the children's bedroom. I leaned over Harry's bed and shook him gently. His face became fierce and he rolled away from me, trying to straddle the wall and save his sleep. "Harry," I whispered. "Listen, Harry, wake up."

He rolled back and his eyes opened. "Shhh," I warned and I took his hand and led him from the bed. We went into the living room, where I dimmed the light so that he could open his eyes again.

Harry is a fair child, his coloring like my own, yet paler, as if he has faded. He seemed a little fleshed out with the puffiness of sleep and there were red sleep creases down the side of one cheek and on his neck. I sat on the sofa and pulled him up onto my lap. Not yet really awake, he was soft and pliant. He leaned against my chest, his breath on my throat.

"Harry," I said, "I have to tell you something. Are you listening?"

He sighed, making a small motion with his head.

"Harry," I said, "if I ever did any bad things to you, I didn't mean them. Do you understand? I love you better than anyone. Do you hear me?"

He looked back at me and he didn't answer. But I thought I perceived a new yielding of his body as I held him against me and I was satisfied.

10

After a while, people began to know. Joseph's mother knew with a terrible look of triumph. Joseph knew with a sudden inability to meet my glance when he spoke to me, awed by my close association with horror.

One Sunday I left the boys with him at a playground near our house and I went to visit my mother and father. We sat in their living room, steam piping up from a chorus of radiators. My mother picked at a doily on the arm of the sofa. She stood up and stared at the row of philodendron plants on top of the television set as if she had never seen them before.

"He was always a gentlemen," she said. The most tender of epitaphs. "Do you remember when you were only kids? Do you remember his nice manners?"

My father nodded his head and tapped his fingers on the table next to his chair. "Do you remember when he used to come in on a Sunday and I would cut his hair?"

"Hello Mrs. Stein, good-bye Mrs. Stein. Thank you, please, you're welcome."

"Such thick hair," my father murmured. "Such a good head of hair."

"Tootsie," my mother said, touching my arm. *Maybe, just maybe with modern science . . .*"

"No, Ma," I said. "Don't."

"Everybody dies," my father said with a thoughtful sigh.

"What does that have to do with it?" My mother's eyes were cruel. "What do you know about it?"

Even now, I wondered, she could remember old wrongs and feel new anger. Things that were fresh when I was a child in their house. Words that poured through the wall separating our bedrooms. She had promised never to forgive him and she had kept her word. But I remembered the sounds of them together as well, imagined my mother's clothing dropping to her feet, the white nylon uniform with her name, Rose, imagined that the name blazed through to her very flesh, that my father saw it there as he fell on her breast.

"Ma," I said. "Daddy loves Jay."

"I love him," my father confirmed. His eyes filled with tears and he blew his nose.

"Are you going to tell Mona?" my mother asked.

"I'll have to tell her sometime." I would have to invade Paradise. "Not yet. I don't know. I don't want to do *anything.* I want the whole world to stop."

"Sandy . . ."

"Don't worry, Ma. I talk, talk, talk."

"You don't talk so much," my father observed. "Get it off your chest."

"Thanks, Daddy."

"Do you need money?" he asked.

49

"Not now. We're okay now."

"As soon as you need . . ."

"Thanks, Daddy. I know."

"Well," my mother said. I saw that she was searching her head for a new subject. What could she say that would not be indelicately jovial, or that would not bring us back full circle to Jay? "Well," she said, wringing her hands. "Is anybody hungry?"

11

"Izzy," I said. "Help me."

"I'm a good one to help," she said. But that afternoon she came to visit me. "Look what I did to my own life," she said, taking her coat off.

"You didn't do it."

"That doesn't matter. When it felt like the end of the world for me, everything I did was dumb-ass and useless. Like weeping all day, like psychotherapy, like wanting to kill myself."

"You were abandoned."

"Yeah."

"In a way it was like death."

"In a way it was worse. Just tell me, would you give Jay life, would you let him live, if you had the power, if it was with another woman, with *her* children? Think about it. Where you could only see him on Sundays when he came for your kids?"

"Yes," I said.

51

She looked at me, narrowing her eyes. "Do you have something to drink?" she asked.

We sat in the living room later, facing one another. "Did you really want to?" I asked.

She lifted her head and drained her glass. "Did I really want to what?"

"Did you really want to kill yourself?"

"Sure. Yes. I thought about it a lot. I looked at myself everywhere: in mirrors, upside down in spoons, in the handle of the refrigerator door, in subway windows. I saw that same sad swollen face every time I looked. Goodbye, I said to that face. So long. God, it was sadder than real life. I thought, Eddie will be sorry. Then sometimes I thought, he'll be relieved."

"Did you decide on a method?"

"What difference does that make?"

"Well, I once read that it's really a serious intention if you decide on a method. That shows a genuine desire to carry it out."

Isabel motioned to me for another drink. "Gas," she said dreamily.

We were silent for a while, each with her own mind pictures. I saw Isabel dead in the false cheer of her kitchen with its frilly curtains and its shining pots and pans. It seemed terribly ironic to die deliberately in the very room designated for the nurturing of life, a room with eggs and oranges and milk in it. We drank for a while in silence and then I asked, "Why didn't you do it?"

"Oh, not for the reasons you think. Not for the sake of the kids or because I saw suicide as a futile gesture or a disturbed act. It was the lousy value system that stopped me, the old material greed. I had a bad cold for a few days. I could hardly breathe anyway. I thought, fine, this is a good time. Why not? And sometimes when I looked

52

at my reflection I held my breath for a long time until it burst out of me and I was wheezing and gasping. I thought that I was rehearsing. It was almost thrilling in a way, the anticipation. All day long in that old green bathrobe, shredding and balling up damp tissues in the pockets.

"Then a woman from some place I never heard of, some church or synagogue, I don't even remember, called up and asked if I had any old clothes to donate. '*My* clothes?' I asked. 'Certainly,' she said. 'That would be fine. Anything would be greatly appreciated.' 'What would you do with them?' I asked her.

"She seemed surprised but she explained that the better things were distributed among poor families and that everything else was sold as rags with the proceeds going to good and charitable works.

"It was crazy. I thought of my gray dress. I thought of my yellow sweater with the iris embroidered on the pocket. I thought of some poor woman, illiterate, shoeless, bedraggled, wearing my brown coat with the beaver collar. 'My things!' I said. 'My things!' 'Beg pardon?' the woman said, 'how's that?' and I hung up and got dressed and went to a movie."

"My God," I said. I looked into the bottom of my empty glass.

Izzy jumped forward and filled it, and then hers. She stared at me for a while. "I was always jealous of you," she said.

"Me?"

"Because I wasn't pretty. When we were kids. Because you had blond hair. Oh, how I wanted blond hair! And I was always such a horse."

I remembered that Jay always thought of her as the antithesis of femininity with her shingled haircut and her

big-muscled legs planted in that stolid stance. She reminded him of a gym instructor or a coach and he once
said that he thought she carried a whistle in the canyon between those ballooning breasts. But I had known Isabel
for a long time, back when her adolescent dreams of
being only a wife and a mother seemed so simple and
gently unambitious. After Eddie left, for a long time she
was immobile and sad.

"A nice fat jelly-belly," she said.

I lifted my hand in protest but she waved it away.
"True, true," she insisted. "But then when I saw *her*!
I thought she would look like you, nice bones and all,
small. I was romantic about her. But she looked like
me!" She sighed. "You see, I'm the wrong one to come to
for help. I talked about myself all day."

I thought of all the things I didn't know about her life,
and yet she was my closest friend. Jay and I had closed
ourselves off from other real intimacies. Our own friendship had always been enough. I leaned across the table
and kissed Izzy's cheek. "Listen," I said. "Did you really
go for therapy or did you just think about it?"

"Oh, I went all right," she said. "I certainly went."

I sat forward expectantly but she didn't say anything
else. "Well, did it help?"

"Not me. It certainly didn't help me. You know me,
Sandy. I'm just too hardheaded, too literal. I can't even
take the interpretation of dreams. If I dream of drowning,
I believe that I'm dreaming of drowning. If my husband
needed another woman, I couldn't relate it to his child-
hood, to his mother. Who gives a damn about his mother?
I didn't want to know about his drives and his anxieties.
I only wanted him to stop screwing around."

"Yes," I said.

"*He* wouldn't go. That was the end of that."

54

We sat quietly for a while, reflective, slumped in our seats.

"Sandy, I don't know. Maybe it would help you to get through this. Maybe you should go."

I kicked off my shoes and lay down on the sofa. "I'll go to you," I said. "Sit up and look a little Freudian."

Izzy laughed. "What are you doing?"

"Shhhh. Quiet. I'll tell you my life story."

"I think you're crazy."

"Certainly. Zat's vy I am here, Doctor."

Izzy lit a cigarette. "Tell me about your childhood," she said.

I shut my eyes and began to tell her. I told her first thoughts and first memories. I told her about my mother and my father and my first remembered image of the world. I forgot about the room we were in. I talked about death and love and anxiety and about all the hazards of being alive. I talked about awareness and denial and vanity and sorrow and happiness.

I talked and talked and the sun went out of the room and finally I looked up and saw that Isabel was asleep in her chair, one leg twisted under the other. She snored gently and her hands were opened palm up on the arms of the chair. I stood and tiptoed past her feeling slightly lightheaded but strangely refreshed.

12

Joseph was slouched on the sofa with Paul between his knees. I was preparing to leave for the hospital when the telephone rang. It was Jay calling to speak to the children. Paul rushed to the phone. "Daddy? *Me!*" he said, with a smile of triumph. "I'm watching television with Joseph. *Joseph!*" he yelled.

"Shh," I cautioned, trying to calm him with motions of my hand.

But Paul's voice was strident, his color high. "I have a new truck," he screamed. "I have Sugar Pops!"

I tapped Paul's shoulder but he shrugged my hand away. "I'm watching cartoons, Daddy. I'm going to the park."

I tapped him again. "Tell Daddy, I miss you," I whispered.

"I miss you!" Paul shrieked in the same falsetto and I sighed. I called Harry from the bedroom. "Daddy is on the telephone. He wants to talk to you."

Harry walked with slow deliberation. After a moment

Paul relinquished the telephone. "Hello," Harry said, and this time I could hear Jay's voice filtered through the receiver.

"Fine," Harry said. "Yes." He sat down in a chair, resting his elbow on its arm. "Fine," he said again. "Okay." He moved the telephone to his other hand.

I waved at him. "Tell Daddy about the movie." I mouthed the words.

"Yes," Harry said, into the phone. "I am."

I waved more wildly. I hissed, "Tell Daddy *something*. Tell him what you've been doing."

Harry wouldn't look at me.

Oh tell him, I thought. At least tell him that he is a good father. Tell him you will remember his face when last seen, that you love him, that you're happy to be his product and his continuity.

But Harry held the telephone out to me. "Daddy wants to talk to you," he said, and he went out of the room.

Yet later, at the hospital, Jay had a special radiance when he talked about the children. He spoke about his telephone conversation with them as if it had been witty and memorable. Then he asked me to buy them presents from him at the hospital gift shop.

Of all the places in the hospital, all the cold and clinical places that project mystery and fear, the gift shop filled me with the greatest sense of dread. Here is where we come eventually for solace, to the *things* in life, wrapped in gift paper. It is the same gift shop in every hospital in the world. There are the browsers, who touch things and put them down again with gloved hands, who wonder at the myriad offerings, at the possibility of their distraction, and at the same time uneasily consider that they may be overpriced. There are the stuffed animals, unpleasantly stiff and coarse to the touch, artificial flowers and plants imitating life in plastic pots. There are key chains and plaques with mottoes, inspirational books about friendship, love, and faith. There are games and puzzles and gifts specifically designed for hospital use, shaving mirrors from which my own face loomed, magnified, and oversized plumed pens, inscribed GET WELL SOON! I thought, here are the true ruins, and in despair I chose a stuffed giraffe for Paul and a kangaroo for Harry. I was waiting at the cash register to pay for them when a man said, "I've been thinking about you."

I looked at him, puzzled, and he laughed. "Sandy?"

"Yes."

He was a big man, ruddy, and with thick graying hair. "Do you remember me?" he asked. "In the parking lot?"

"Of course," I said, looking for his name in my head. "Francis," I said finally, with relief.

He squeezed my arm. "Good girl!" He looked down at the toys in my arms. "For your kids?"

"Yes," remembering that cold night and the homely comfort of the station wagon and his voice.

"Well," I said. "What are you doing here?"

"I'm visiting a buddy. Someone from the office. The same guy actually. I had to bring him some papers . . ."

I handed the stuffed animals and some money to the cashier and Francis waited until I had the packages. He walked out into the lobby with me, where children not permitted on the upper floors waited restlessly to be taken home. Families whispered their private news in corners. A woman was asleep in a molded chair, with two shopping bags held in the slack grip of her knees.

"I'm glad that I have this chance to thank you," I said to Francis. "And you were right. Nobody can do anything to make it better. It's just that now I can talk about it."

"How long does he have?"

"Weeks. Maybe months. See, I can talk about it as if it isn't true."

"You have to protect yourself. You have to do something to get through it."

"I don't have to do anything. Things happen no matter what I do."

"I know. You look thin. Are you eating? Do you take care of yourself?"

I felt uneasy, almost threatened by his concern. I shrugged. "I'm all right."

"Could I buy you a cup of coffee? Could we sit down and talk for a while?"

It was not an unreasonable suggestion. Coffee. Facing a man across a table, someone healthy and stable and interested. But what was his interest? I looked up, trying to assess him, but his face had that same intense and friendly expression. He was giving, and asking for nothing back. Yet I felt the way I do with handsome and insistent salesmen. Drugged, mesmerized by the sales pitch. Afraid that I will weaken and buy something I don't want, couldn't possibly use, for the sake of the transaction itself. "No," I said, shaking my head. "I'm tired. My baby-sitter has to be in early on school nights. This is for the children from him—from Jay." I raised the gift packages. "I want to give this to them tonight."

Francis laughed. "You have a lot of reasons."

"All true."

"All true," he echoed. He walked alongside me as I went out into the parking lot. His stride was long and athletic and I had to walk quickly to keep up with him. "You're here every day," he said. It wasn't a question.

"Yes."

"It becomes a way of life after a while," he said. "My mother died of cancer. She died in slow motion and my father forgot what he had done with his days before she was sick."

"I know."

We had come to my car. "Don't forget who you are," he said, and I felt a great impatience to get away. Suddenly his sympathy was a burden, his friendly scrutiny painful.

He put his hand on the roof of the car and leaned toward me as I sat there. "If you need . . ." he began.

The salesman, confident, intimate, offering easy terms, no cost, no obligation. I put the key into the ignition. "No no," I insisted, and I pressed my foot on the accelerator, drowning out the sound of his voice.

". . . if you ever do," I heard him say, and then I released the brake and drove away.

13

For three years Jay had been compiling material for a photographic essay on life in the city. He worked on it slowly, with the pace of a natural process. He kept everything—the photographs he thought he would include, and a growing manuscript of captions—in a folder in a drawer in our bedroom. The script was simple and artless: the dialogue of the people in the photographs, the names and numbers of the streets. Jay said that even if he never published it, even if he didn't finish it, the effort seemed to be the proper atonement for all the meaningless crap he recorded for television.

He would lay the prints out across the floor of the living room and try to arrange them in some sequence. It became a Sunday morning project and the children, in their pajamas, pretended to help. "Put this one *here*, Daddy."

"Okay. Okay, honey, just wait a minute now." He was distracted, and he hardly noticed them, but his hand reached out anyway, separate from his consciousness, and he rubbed their heads and tickled their feet. He studied his photographs the way Old World Jews would study the Talmud. They knew it by heart, but there was always a possibility of discovering something new, some hidden and revelatory meaning.

They're large photographs and it was startling to walk by and be assaulted by those images. The city seen through Jay's camera has an arrested look, as if motion has been artificially stopped, and then begun again the moment we look away. Of course he was mostly concerned with the people, with their faces, with the intricate composition in space of their figures on a city street. Half shutting my eyes, so that the lashes formed a veil to blur my vision, I looked through Jay's folder, almost afraid now to encounter his perception of the world. But after a while I opened my eyes and looked at the photographs closely again, bringing into focus his credulousness, his concern, his tender insight. I turned the photos one after the other in a parade of evidence, and the people looked back from crumbling and elegant streets, surprised to find themselves there, in that very moment, for some mystical purpose, alive. And there was the dumb look of lean dogs crouching in city streets, tramps of the world, and the leavings of garbage and graffiti, and the *idea* of people suggested even in the empty geometry of city landscapes.

Yet he was never really satisfied with what he had done. Once, when I made a fuss over a new batch of prints, he said, "Yeah, but I don't think it's what I really want. I want to get inside . . ."

"My God, you're a madman," I said. "Jay, these are *good!*" I picked up a photograph of a black woman and her family eating their dinner at a small square table. She looked polished, as if she were made of some durable life-resistant wood. Yet the whole photograph had a dusty granular quality to it, as if it were very old and had nothing to do with these glittering, accelerated times. "Matthew Brady could have taken this," I said.

Jay looked pleased then. "Do you think so, Sandy? That's what I want to do, get across the idea of ongoing history. You know, we're all old, young, dying, dead, resurrected."

But it wasn't really ever enough. For instance you can't show poverty the easy way, with torn underwear hanging on frayed clotheslines. Conditions of the spirit are evasive, maybe even unphotographable.

I brought the folder and the cameras he had asked for to the hospital. Jay and Martin photographed one another, nurses who pretended petulance, other patients, and the view from the window of their room. When I came to visit again, Martin took my picture as I entered the room, and I worried later what face I had been wearing for posterity.

Martin looked through the folder over and over again. "God, this is beautiful stuff, Jay," he said. "This is the way I always felt about the city, like as bad as it is, it's the only place where you can live a *real* life. Do you know what I mean? Someday I'm going to do portraits, nothing else. Eyes kill me."

Jay winked at me over Martin's bent head.

When I was home again that night, I looked into the mirror at my own eyes. Did I expect to find in them some mystical continuation of our lives, or even a permanent reflection of what had already been? I stared, moving closer and closer, watching the starburst of yellow open around the pupils until my breath fogged the mirror.

14

Fatigue was Jay's main complaint. He went to bed fatigued and he woke unrefreshed as if sleep had been an arduous labor. Dr. Block had said something vague to him about all those tests—something about metabolic disorder and low-grade infection. Jay was no fool—he wasn't getting well, and yet he made no demands to know more. I believed then that he *did* know and that it was just a matter of acknowledgment, of giving consent and embracing terror.

Cautiously we examined one another's knowledge and we mumbled words about the mysteries of the human body. Yet we did not say even one word that suggested good-bye. We stayed close to the room and Martin's voice, avoiding any private place in which to lay out our feelings. We tried not to speak in very clinical terms either, keeping flesh in its proper place as an object of love. Yet when we spoke about the children, grief and longing showed plainly on his face.

It was decided that I would bring them to the parking lot of the hospital so that Jay could see them from the window of the room opposite his. It would be an odd excursion for the children: to be at the hospital, but not allowed upstairs, to see Jay, but only as a remote hazy figure they could not really identify. Would they remember him?

I helped them with their snowsuits and scarves and we drove to the hospital. I kept thinking, they're very young, they won't even remember this. What could I recall from those distant days when I was only three-four-five-years old? And what had I invented because it filled an empty space and satisfied longing?

Paul was just coming out of babyhood. I looked at him quickly as I drove, at the baby softness of his features. You could not imagine bone under such delicate perfect flesh. His fingers were still tapered, cushioned at the base, and I saw that they were dirty, that there was dirt under the short papershell pink of his nails. He sighed and pushed them out of sight, into his mouth.

He would look like Jay, I realized with a thrill of terror. Jay had looked like that when he was a baby. Those deep-set eyes, that sweet curling mouth. Only the flattened bridge of his nose saved him from beauty. People would say, "You look just like your father." He would remind me, as his features, his final self emerged from this compressed beginning of a man. Maybe his voice would be like Jay's too. They learn language from us. A year ago Paul had only a few words and he listened to us and then he began to string them together. He watched Jay and imitated gesture too. He tried to throw a ball, to run, to hold a fork the way his father did. Sometimes he shuffled through the apartment, endearingly awkward, wearing Jay's shoes. And when Jay winked at him, Paul would try desperately to wink back, his mouth working, his whole face contorted with the effort and the ecstacy of imitation. "That's good, honey," Jay told him. "You've almost got it now."

But Paul would not consciously remember this day or the ones before it. There would only be a fragmented series of events, confused and distorted. A sense of the car's motion perhaps, the pleasant joggling reminiscent of the cradle, and the peculiar taste of his own fingers. Going to see someone once, somewhere, and then coming home again.

But Harry would be different. Five was a more established age anyway. He could write his own name in broad uncertain letters and he would be going to school in the fall. And Harry was like me, a hoarder of experience. He stood on the back seat of the car on his knees, looking through the window at the rushing landscape, gasping lightly at the corpse of a car-flattened animal and saying nothing. I was jealous for him because his brother had been favored by fate and would be more lovable for all time to come. Suddenly I wished that he too could look like Jay instead of like me, that I could will some of Jay's gestures and features onto him, as if I were dividing property fairly and squarely among the heirs.

Then we were at the hospital and they waited in the car while I went into the lobby. I called Jay on the telephone and he sounded breathless, excited. "The kids are here now? Great! Just give me a minute, Sandy."

"Which window?" I asked, and he said, "Three over from your left. Hey, you'll know me. I'll be the one with the red carnation."

"Ha ha," I said, close to tears, but willing to play the game.

Then I went back to the car and took the children out

66

onto the melting filthy ice of the parking lot. "Where's Daddy?" Paul asked.

We looked up at the wall of windows, where figures and shadows appeared and disappeared. Then I saw him at the assigned place. At least I saw a man, appearing crazily tall and thin, who lifted his arm in the bold gesture of a monarch saluting his kingdom.

"There he is! There!" I said, pointing, waving frantically.

"I don't see him," Harry said.

"Up *there*. Do you see, where the ladies are and the flowers? Now look up a little higher. Do you see the man waving?"

Harry put one hand across his brow, shielding his eyes from the winter sun. "I see him," he said, almost without expression.

"Daddy!" Paul yelled.

"He can't hear you. The windows are shut." But then I forgot too and when I waved again I said, "Jay."

Another figure appeared beside him. A nurse? A patient?

We were standing and waving like fools, like people who walk toward the movie camera, closer, closer, balloon-faced and self-conscious, saying soundless words.

I thought of Jay up there willing to admire us, to *adore* us for old time's sake. But I wanted to entertain him, to dazzle him with the virtuosity of our style. He was entitled to that at least. And I wasn't even sure that the children had really seen him, no matter what they said. They were restless, starting to shiver. God, it was *boring* for them to be there, where nothing happened, where all sound was cut off by glass, and everything, even our best intentions, was diminished by distance. I looked around, desperate for inspiration, for props, something to give Jay his money's worth.

"Boys," I said. "Let's show Daddy the snow. Let's make snowballs." We all bent, trying to scoop up the slush, scraping at patches of ice. "Look," I cried, throwing into the air a thin wet mass that immediately splattered at my feet.

"The snow is no good," Harry said. "My hands are cold."

"Watch out now," I said, trying to roll another one that began to melt in my glove and slip down into the sleeve of my coat. "I'll race you," I said to Harry. "I'll race you to that green car. On your mark, get set, go!" And I began to run, slipping on icy places, regaining my balance and running again. I watched Harry, saw him with his chest thrust out, saw the blurred locomotion of his arms and legs, saw Paul, encumbered by the swaddling of his snow-suit and his need to stop and shout every few minutes, "Wait for me, I *can't*!"

How did they appear to Jay? Foreshortened and distant, two small bright spots of color, once known. People stepped from a car, carrying plants. They stopped to watch us, and to let us pass.

I looked up at the window, was struck with vertigo, and had to look down again. Harry passed me, his eyes popping with the effort. I heard his panting and the slapping of his boots.

We ran in and out between the parked cars, in some crazy choreography. Paul was whining, "Stop it, I can't."

I was exhausted and the cold stung at my face and hands, and yet I felt invigorated. This is what it's all about, I thought. Motion. The essence of life. "Huh huh," I said, almost out of breath, and forcing myself to go on, until Harry passed me again and I found that I was only running in place.

I looked up again slowly at Jay and saw that people had appeared at a dozen windows, waving, pointing to us. We were a veritable parade of life, as if we carried banners proclaiming ourselves, and I imagined ticker tapes and cheers falling on our heads like new snow.

15

The cold began innocently enough: a few sneezes shattering night silence, an ache in the throat only vaguely different from the one I felt every day now. But by morning it couldn't be denied or disguised and a cold was a dangerous weapon to bring to the hospital.

Dr. Block was hearty. Here was something he could handle, something needing nose drops and cough syrup and a few kind words. For good measure he prescribed an all-purpose antibiotic as well. "Take a little vacation," he said. "Your resistance is low."

He meant a vacation from vigilance and grief, but I chose to listen with a literal ear and I decided that I would go away, if only for a day. Izzy said that she would be happy to have the boys stay at her apartment. I left them there in the morning and then I took the subway to the bus station. Looking back as I walked to the corner, I could see a mixture of faces at the window, her kids and mine, as if they were seeing me off on some long and doubtful journey.

But I was only going to New Jersey. The bus station seemed the right place for my departure because it is so much more solemn than an airport. There is a distinct lack of adventure and joy. For one thing, people at bus stations are poorer than the people at airports. Their clothing is less festive and their luggage is shabby and dull.

It was easy to imagine the contents of those pseudo-leather cardboard cases. More of the same dresses and jackets that the passengers themselves were wearing, in lifeless rayon that creases easily. Underwear with meager lace that shreds when laundered. The old ladies carried corsets rolled like diplomas, and Bibles, and reserves of food slyly hidden next to their shoes. The men had those magazines that are sold in stores on 42nd Street, to be taken out again in some drab hotel, hopeful they will revive fantasies and ward off loneliness.

There were many black people, and people carrying their belongings from one place to another with suspicious care, straddling the suitcases when they paused, as if they were astride horses.

At the entrance aisle to my bus, other passengers clutching tickets and shopping bags called back and forth about newspapers and babies and not forgetting to write. Good-bye, they called. Good-bye. We boarded the bus. In front of me a thin woman held an infant on her lap. She kept looking through the window and whispering with grotesque lip movements. "Defrost the refrigerator," she said. "Don't forget to defrost the refrigerator. The re-frig-er-a-tor," and then she held the baby up and waved its little hand and the bus began to move in a fury of noise and exhaust fumes.

I had never been to Atlantic City in the winter, though my mother and father and I had always gone there for our two-week vacation. A sign hung on the front door of the beauty shop. CLOSED FOR VACATION. WILL REOPEN ON JULY 23RD.

My father would be frenetic with plans, while my mother laid our vacation clothing in little piles on their bed. He said that we would go swimming, that the waves would be taller than the Empire State Building. His arms became the waves, reaching above his head and then swooping down, surrounding me as I shrieked hoarsely for joy, as I would shriek again in the real ocean and hang onto the flesh of his back. My mother smiled too and hummed tuneless songs as she folded bathing suits and pajamas.

Just before the bus started, a woman walked down the aisle. She was huge, fluid as an amoeba, flesh displacing flesh. Her breasts were so immense, so stretched from their starting place, that released from their hammocks they might slap against her knees. Inside tan leather shoes, her feet spread to capacity, the way that a goldfish grows to suit its confinement. I knew somehow that she would sit next to me. She hurled a small bag onto the luggage rack and then she ducked her head and lowered herself into the seat. Puffing frantic little breaths, her eyes rolling with the effort, she sat there, pale and quivering. I was jammed against the window but somehow it was not unpleasant. "Someone has to get me," she said. "Are you traveling alone?"

"Yes," I said. She looked expectant and I realized that she waited for me to return the question. "And you?" I asked.

She nodded, shutting her eyes for a moment. "Alone."

The bus picked up speed and I looked through the window, saw the rush of landscape in a continuous colored ribbon, and then I looked back at her again.

"Alone," she said again, this time with a significant wink. "My father died. I just switched off from a bus from Beaufort. In North Carolina, you know? That's where he was born. That's where I buried him."

I thought that she might have literally buried him herself, digging up the earth, tossing the coffin as she had tossed the suitcase, and then tamping the turned soil with those great feet.

"He trapped me for thirty-one years. Do I look thirty-one?"

She could have been fifty.

"I have this glandular condition," she said.

Oh yes, I knew about that glandular condition. I knew what ailed that great floured chicken, how she ate her secret food, those dolly lips opening, cartoon style, into canyons. She ate instead of weeping, then she ate because she had not wept, and then she ate *while* she wept and everything had a salty taste.

"That's too bad," I said.

"He was a tyrant," she said. "He pinned me to the house, like a butterfly to a card? On account of him, I never had a man in my life. In no sense of the word."

I rolled my eyes in sympathy.

"I might as well've been locked behind bars. He was a very religious man. They all are," she added vaguely. "He said that God would reward me. Now I guess he has. When he died, when I heard the rattle and all? I held the shaving mirror up to his lips. Nothing. I held a match close to the hairs in his nose. I stuck a fork into his arm. He never once moved. He never said a word. Now I've

73

got my own life. Now that he's gone, I can do whatever I want. It's never too late, they say."

"It's never too late," I echoed, hating the irony of those words.

But she smiled as if I had said something original and exactly to the point. "So I'm going to start a new life," she said. "I'm going out to California."

I started and she laughed. "Oh, I'm not on the wrong bus or anything. First I'm going to Jersey to stay with my sister for a while. I'm going to work in her husband's diner in Brigantine for a while. To help them out—my sister has trouble with her kidney. Then I'm going to start my new life. Of course I'll have to get rid of some of this." She rolled rubbery flesh against my arm. "Where are you going?" she asked.

"Atlantic City," I said. "To visit my aunt."

"Oh that's nice. But you ought to go in the summertime. You could go swimming."

And then I remembered swimming again, the pull and thrust of the surf, and my mother waiting with towels like a handmaiden at the shore as my father and I trudged out onto the sand. I remembered the particular taste of sandwiches eaten on the beach and the brilliant striped wheel of the umbrella above us and the smell of salt and fish.

The woman next to me said, "Maybe I'll go to Washington, D.C., before I go to California. Maybe I could get a job in the government. I mean after I lose this weight. I saw where some man in a hospital lost three hundred pounds. Of course he must have been enormous. He slept downstairs in the parlor for twenty years. For twenty years he never saw the upstairs."

We were both silent in contemplation of that. I sneezed twice and blew my nose.

"A cold," she said sadly. "You want to take care of that. My father began with a cold. You want to drink tea and lemon and honey. Burning hot. You want to inhale the steam."

We each ate an Oh Henry! bar from a six-pack she had in her purse and then she put her head back and shut her eyes. Her face told me that she had thrust herself into the glorious future. Her father flew on paper wings toward the heaven reserved for righteous fools. Weight slipped from her like snakeskin. She was in the pages of the *Ladies' Home Journal,* looking as stylish as Irene Rich. She could do anything. Anybody could do anything.

I was left alone in my corner of the seat. In my head I found a picture of Jay as I had seen him last and I felt the seat grow more cramped as I expanded in sorrow. Jay's hair, Indian-black against the pillow, the flesh of his face and neck, ivory-white and vulnerable as a saint's. Then I thought of other earlier times when we would lie embraced and about the human need to touch and be touched as if it had been an original idea of ours. Myself tracing the flattened bridge of Jay's nose, the long and elegant bones of his body, and the renewable surprise of his sex filling my hand. How lucky we were that we had invented one another, that we had those bodies to use as tools of love, that we had a bed in which to be together.

Like a penny movie, parts of our lives rolled behind my eyes. The dailiness seemed like something that might go on forever and ever. How slowly we did everything: ate our food and walked and picked things up and put them down again. I saw Jay's hand on the steering wheel of the car, and his shimmering shadow behind the glass door of the shower. I wouldn't be able to stand the simplest things anymore.

In the bus, my seatmate moved, bringing me back to

the moment. "I never had a man," she said wonderingly. "Not in any sense of the word."

"There is only one sense of the word," I told her.

"By golly," she said. "I can do anything I want now. I'm free as a bird."

I turned to smile at her in encouragement, but her face had collapsed into folds of grief, and tears ran through the maze. I took her hand and she squeezed mine. Then she fell asleep and she didn't wake up again until we came into the bus station in Atlantic City. I held her hand all the way. In Atlantic City I stood on the platform and waved. She had moved next to the window and we shouted "Good luck, good luck," to each other. She waved her hand at me and she was clutching an Oh Henry! wrapper.

The colors were only variations of gray—filthy white in the distance above the ocean, gray towers of the hotels like cathedrals along the boardwalk.

But I remembered color, in a defiant display, and I wondered if the facades had faded, washed pale by the dampness and the salt. Even the beach, once the yellow of sandboxes, was gray. No umbrellas now, no sunning bodies in the absurd colors of summer clothing. The wind blew in theatrical rushes, pulling at the sleeves of my coat like impatient children. I thought that I would probably get pneumonia standing on the boardwalk in the very arms of winter. I sneezed, I coughed, I turned my face directly into the wind and shut my eyes. But I knew that it was I who was theatrical and not the wind. If I wanted to die, there were easier and less devious ways to accomplish it. But I didn't even entertain that idea on any but the most romantic level. Seeing myself *after* the fact, drowned, with splayed fingers of wet hair worn like a crown, or poisoned, with no more finality than Snow White, rising again and again from the soft coffin bed. Saw myself only *later* with the poor white feet of Caravaggio's Christ, but never, never in the agony of the cross. So I wanted to live in the face of everything. To breathe in and out, sneeze, sleep, wake (ah, yes, to wake), even to suffer the end of Jay. Anything, not to suffer the end of me. I hugged myself, partly because of the cold that seemed to enter my bones and partly in celebration of my own flesh. Now I wanted to be warm again, to be fed, to talk to someone, simply to continue.

We had not always stayed at the same hotel: my mother's idea, I suppose, to keep my father on the move and away from lasting relationships. One of the hotels had been torn down, and rising from the ruins was a low modern motel. Another was boarded up and shut for the winter. But a third, thrillingly familiar, was open to the public. I wondered who came there to bask in the cold winter sun. There had been only a few figures on the boardwalk, hunched against the wind, and at least one of them had been a derelict, stumbling, perhaps in the delusion that it was summer.

Who lives here? I wanted to shout, as I entered the lobby of the hotel. Everyone there was old. An old man slept in an overstuffed chair that seemed to embrace him. Two old women sat poised on the edge of a love seat. Even the desk clerk was stooped and wrinkled, and he rested his head against the quiet wall of the switchboard. It seemed to be merely a stage set, a place on which the actors, my mother and father and myself, would soon appear. On the worn red carpet of the staircase, perhaps, in woolen bathing suits and beach robes, with pail and shovel and newspaper and lunch basket and towels and blankets; so encumbered as to almost stagger.

Why had I never asked Jay to come here with me so that I could show him a small piece of my history? He always used imagery in his photographs as a silent language. He would have understood. One memory is worth a thousand words.

I knew that I came back here now because I believed it had been a place where my parents and I had truly loved one another, where we had been a perfect triumvirate of love. This was safe ground in my mind, where somehow we had been all and enough for my father. I could remember no quarrels. I was even included in their room to lie on a cot unfolded by a colored maid who seemed to approve of us. Had it all been in my imagination? It didn't matter. It was only important that I believed it, that I continued to believe it even in the face of all evidence.

I walked around the edges of the lobby, saw that the barbershop and the gift store were closed, saw the arrows that pointed to the direct passage to the beach, saw the paintings (the same, the same) of waterfowl, of sheep, of brown ships on a brown sea.

The dining room was open for lunch. Only a small cluster of tables was set, still with white cloths and frosted pitchers of water and silverware that would be heavy in the hand. White napkins stood in pyramids at every setting. It was early and only one table was occupied. An elderly woman sat there, wearing a fur-collared coat. She held the massive menu in front of her as it were a hymnal.

There were no waiters in the dining room. I stood in the doorway and waited and then the woman looked up over her pince-nez and nodded, as if she expected me.

I nodded too and even smiled. How would a voice sound in the quiet of that room?

She raised her water glass to her lips and drank. Then she cleared her throat in three harsh sounds and said, "Are you meeting someone?"

I shook my head. "No."

"Would you care to join me?"

I walked through the hoop of light thrown by the crystal chandelier. "Thank you," I said. When I removed my coat and sat down, she handed the menu to me.

"Your nose is all red," she said accusingly.

I raised a wrinkled tissue to it. "A cold."

"Soup," she said. "Fluids."

Then, as if on cue, the waiter came on the sides of his collapsed feet, and teetered above us until we ordered.

It seemed that she would accept me without question, as if I were Alice, entering her world through a dream.

"I came here as a child," I said.

"I came here before then," she answered.

"It seems smaller now."

"Everything shrinks."

"I know. Schoolrooms. Old houses."

"I came here on my honeymoon," she said, and I knew that her husband was long dead.

"I came here with my mother and father." Somehow she had aroused a competition between us.

"We had filet of sole for our wedding lunch. The manager sent a bottle of wine."

"We were very happy here," I said. Was it true? I remembered ordering food in the dining room. It was a serious business. The waiters came to know us and would wait a long time before they came to the table to take our order. My father would say, "The veal looks good. Chops sound nice."

My mother would nod. "How about the filet of had-dock?"

"I don't know," he'd answer. "I don't feel like fish. Do you want soup?"

"Do you?" my mother would ask.

"I don't know," my father would say, and on and on through the vegetables du jour, the salad dressing, the beverage, the dessert.

Now the waiter came with bowls of soup in trembling hands.

She lifted her spoon and said, "I've come back here every year for forty-five years." Her chin was raised triumphantly and I knew that the contest was over.

"Then you were here when I was a child."

"There were so many children." She dismissed them with a wave of her ringed fingers. "My children hate this place. They always say, 'Why do you come back here? It's rotting. It will fall into the sea.'"

We ate our soup in silence for a while.

Then she put her spoon down. "Once, last year, I think it was, I was eating breakfast right here, and a woman came into the dining room. She looked deranged. Her coat was buttoned wrong. Her hat came over her eyes. She began to shout. 'How can you sit here eating rolls and butter when children are starving all over the world?'

"'Are you hungry?' I asked her.

"'It's your decadence that's killing them, that's swelling their bellies!'

"The manager came running from the kitchen. 'I'm an old woman,' I said. 'I hardly enjoy my food anymore.'

"But she only repeated herself. 'It's your decadence that's killing them!' The manager waved his arms at her. 'Out! Out!' he shouted.

"'Just listen,' I told her, 'my teeth don't even fit right. I can hardly chew. They irritate my gums.'

" 'Decadence, decadence!' she said. The manager grabbed her sleeve and pulled her toward the door. On the way out she knocked over water glasses and she took rolls from the last table."

"The world is changing," I said, selfish, meaning *my* world.

"It's true, though," she said. "I can't eat a steak anymore."

"People are desperate."

"I can't even breathe well. I sleep on three pillows."

The waiter came and removed the soup bowls and brought the main course.

"I don't know," she said. "Next year I might go to Miami."

Out on the boardwalk again, fortified by the food, I saw two brown horses carrying riders along the shore. I walked past closed amusement places and frozen custard stands. At the barred entrance to the steel pier, shredding posters announced the world-famous diving horse and Stars! Stars! Stars! The wind lowed and the water licked around the legs of the pier. Coming soon! the posters said. A Galaxy of Stars For Your Entertainment!

Further down the boardwalk, a voice beckoned from a sheltered arcade. "THIS IS THE PLACE FOLKS HERE IT IS COME IN TO CURL YOUR TOES TICKLE YOUR FANCY AND WARM YOUR NOSE THAT'S FANCY F-A-N-C-Y NO OFFENSE TO THE LADIES THIS IS THE FREE-EST SHOW ON EARTH GATHER AROUND ME CHILDREN BECAUSE I HAVE TO HAVE YOUR CLOSE AND UNDIVIDED ATTENTION!"

Obediently I went toward the sound of the voice and saw in the square of yellow light that others were already gathered. It was the same sort of auction that we had attended on summer nights years ago and I remembered that I always sat up near the front, innocent and free from the possibility of coercion, while my parents would cautiously sit in the last row.

Once the auctioneer had given me a plastic letter opener inscribed Willie J. Parnes 25 Years Atlantic City N.J. "THIS IS ONLY THE BEGINNING FOLKS ONLY THE BEGINNING OF THE GIVEAWAY TRUST ME IF YOU'LL ONLY TRUST ME MOVE A LITTLE CLOSER HONEY I DON'T BITE CHOMP CHOMP," and he held a set of clicking false teeth in his hand. Then he gave me a small American flag and I waved it in triumph at my parents, who moved closer and closer, a row at a time, as if they were ambushing the enemy.

They may have bought other things but I remember a radio, compact and ivory, that stood on our refrigerator at home after the vacation. Voices and music faded and blared, faded and blared, interrupted by fits of static for which my father beat it as if trying to revive someone in a terrible spasm of coughing. "Damn radio, damn radio! Oh, that bastard!" And one memory of the summer was less than perfect.

A small knot of people were in the auction room now, sitting together up front as if they were warming themselves at a hearth. A black woman smiled at me and removed her massive handbag from the folding chair next to hers, and I sat down.

"He just beginning," she said. It was as if we were in church and I had not missed the opening remarks of the minister.

I wondered briefly what I was doing there then, as if I had been mugged and shanghaied and was just struggling to come to myself again. I thought, I should be home now dragging myself through some domestic rites, folding clothes warm from the dryer, making soup, chasing dust, concentrating on Jay, on Jay.

And then the auctioneer began again, his voice as soothing and hypnotic as one's own pulse and heartbeat. "OKAY OKAY," he said, his mouth too close to the microphone. "THIS IS THE RIGHT PLACE WITH NO OBLIGATION ABSOLUTELY NO OBLIGATION EXCEPT TO CONTROL YOURSELF AND NOT WALK OUT WITH EVERY INCREDIBLE BARGAIN THAT IS GOING TO MAKE YOUR EYES POP RIGHT OUT OF YOUR HEAD JUST TO WARM YOU UP A LITTLE BIT AND SHOW YOU THAT YOU HAVE NOTHING TO FEAR EXCEPT FOR THE GUY SITTING NEXT TO YOU I'M GIVING A FEW THINGS AWAY THAT'S RIGHT DON'T CLEAN OUT YOUR EARS MOTHER *GIVING* AWAY AS AN ACT OF FAITH AND FRIENDSHIP MOVE A LITTLE CLOSER DON'T MOVE AWAY WHEN THE MAN IS GIVING THINGS AWAY WHEN HE IS MOVED TO THE ACT OF GIVING HOW CAN YOU SEE MY FRIEND?" (to a man just entering and seating himself in the last row). "DON'T BE A STRANGER IN PARADISE MY FRIEND BUT COME CLOSER AND GET IN ON A GOOD THING."

The man in the last row smiled and folded his arms.

"OKAY YOU BE THE SERGEANT AT ARMS AND SEE THAT NOBODY TRIES TO LEAVE HA HA." A fan of ball-point pens opened in his hand. "A LITTLE LEGERDEMAIN SONNY," (this to a small black boy who buried his face against his father's coat). "THAT'S BIG FOR MAGIC COME ON SONNY PICK A COLOR ANYTHING YOU LIKE BECAUSE IT'S ALL YOURS WITH NO OBLIGATION TAKE IT TAKE IT."

The father prodded and poked and the boy finally reached one small hand out and grasped the pen nearest to it. The father immediately took it from him and wrote with it on the back of an envelope.

"PENS THAT WRITE NOTHING BUT THE BEST HERE IN ATLANTIC CITY WHERE QUALITY IS FIRST AND FOREMOST PENS THAT WRITE UNDER WATER UNDER THE INFLUENCE TOASTERS THAT TOAST FOUR SLICES OF BREAD AT ONE TIME WITH A MAGICOLOR DIAL A BUILT-IN BRAIN THAT TELLS YOU WHEN YOUR TOAST IS READY RADIOS THAT FIT INTO THE PALM OF YOUR HAND BLENDERS THAT CHOP MIX BLEND GRIND WHIP BEAT SADISTIC BLENDERS AND PENS THAT WRITE FOR YOU AND YOU AND YOU"

I snuffled and felt my head nodding pleasantly, almost in rhythm with his voice. I had a right to be there after all, to have a little peace, the way a sick child has a right to absent herself from school and luxuriate in her mother's care.

"You sick?" the woman next to me asked.

"Yes. Only a cold."

"Cold, huh? Jello for that, before it sets. Nice good hot jello clean out the passages."

I rose from the seat, still nodding, and she patted my arm. "Jello," she said again, and I lurched out into the gray light of the boardwalk.

My head felt clogged with the cold and with crowding thoughts as I sat on a bench in the bus station waiting to end my pilgrimage. There was a large family sitting near me. The children, uniformly pale and restless, banged their heels against the lower slats of the bench and swatted listlessly at each other.

"Stop it," the mother said from time to time, pinching the arm of the child who happened to be nearest to her. "Stop it for Christ's sake."

The father dozed, snored, and woke occasionally, looking surprised to find himself there, with that particular wife and those squirming battling children. He'd rub his eyes and grunt, then settle his buttocks against the unyielding wood of the bench and sleep again.

A loudspeaker announced the departure and arrival of buses—"Ventnor. Margate. Ocean City." The father was startled awake again and he turned his glazed eyes to look at me. *Now* what? his face said. He lit a cigarette and all the children vied for the honor of blowing out the match, spittle flying, sparkling as dew on the fine hair of my arm, on my pocketbook. "Watch out for the lady, stupid!" Father blew smoke rings to encircle the frail waist of the youngest girl. Mother laughed, leaned over for a puff, and gave the cirgarette back, lipstick-marked and moist. Oh, how dare they be so intimate in the face of everything?

Their bus was announced and they rose at once like a flock of noisy birds. The last boy ran, tripping across my feet, and his mother yanked his arm with a pull that might have wrenched it from its socket and she smiled at me with an endearing smile full of bad teeth and apology.

I yawned, growing luxuriously sleepy, and watched the continuing parade of passengers. A man rushed across the depot floor and his shiny black suitcase flew open. "Oh sh-it!" he cried in true despair and his life's secrets tumbled out as if they had been shot from a cannon. I jumped from the bench to help him and other people stopped too and bent over, picking up the pieces and flinging them back into the open mouth of the suitcase. "Damn lock,"

85

the man muttered, as I touched his jockstrap, his Ivory soap, his *Modern Screen,* his white shirt wrapped in laundry cellophane, his alarm clock, his pamphlets on the new world of computer programming.

"Damn, damn," he said, until the suitcase was filled to overflow. Another man gave him a length of rope and together they bound the suitcase as if it were a resisting prisoner. "Thank you, thank you all!" he called, waving his free arm and running toward the boarding gate. Then they announced the bus to New York.

Boarding the bus and sitting down next to a middle-aged black man, I knew how really tired I was. Jay was dying and I dreamed of a warm bath and food, of cool and perfect sheets. It was as if I were too distracted by life to be concerned with death. Yet when I tried myself once more, letting in the thoughts of darkness and of separation, my heart took terrible plunges. And Jay, surrounded now by the enemy, with the enemy living *inside* him, did he have dreams of soup and bread and other beds for sleep and love instead of for dying?

I began to die then, my mouth and nostrils and ears filling with black earth, and I wanted to pull on the sleeve of the man sitting next to me and confess that I could not stand it, that I would not. But in his dark, African inscrutability, he had turned away from me and fallen asleep.

The bus moved urgently away from the delusions of childhood and back toward the real world. Going away hadn't done very much, after all. Slowed time a little maybe, creating illusions like the ones in a slide show. Maybe I should have gone back to Jay's beginnings instead. What happens to someone's nostalgia when he dies? Jay, near the subway, waiting for his beloved and missing father. Mona, singing in her Bronx kitchen, polishing silver with a pink and pungent cream. Is it possible to reconstruct everything, if you go back? To *change* things? The neighborhoods were all changed. Buildings torn down. Nothing remained constant. Se habla español. Childhood, oh God. Elusive as this moment, now. The movement of the bus rocked and bumped me against the warm arm of the man sitting next to me. I yawned again, and my thoughts became sleepy and disjointed. Back again. Home. Jay. Then I felt myself going under too, into sleep.

The whole journey was made in that sleep and in the bus station in New York again, I went to a telephone booth and called the hospital. The floor nurse said that there were no major changes, that Jay had had a fairly comfortable day. He read a book, she reported. He ate some lunch. Then she connected the call to Jay's room and I heard his voice. "Hello, Sandy?" His voice entered me. Could I say that? Your voice enters me.

He wanted to know about my cold, about the children. "Fine, fine," I said. Your voice enters me.

I told him that I would come to see him as soon as the sniffles were gone. I actually used that word, as professionally cheery as a nurse. Then we blew kisses to one another that fell to their death somewhere in the trunk lines and I hung up.

Back in Isabel's apartment I was surprised to see her ex-husband, Eddie, sitting on the sofa, smoking a pipe. It wasn't Sunday and yet he was there, looking tranquil and domestic, with his younger daughter, Janice, on his lap and Harry nestled close to his side.

In the kitchen Isabel was busy, oven-flushed and happy. It was Janice's birthday and her father had come for the celebration dinner. Paul was wearing a paper birthday hat with a green feather on it. He took my hand and led me to inspect the cake on display next to the refrigerator.

I began to set the table and Eddie came in from the living room, his face lost in the veil of smoke from his pipe. He leaned in the doorway and watched me. "So Jay is having a hard time," he said.

"Yes."

Eddie's pipe made sounds like faulty plumbing and he sucked and sucked at it, as if he were trying to draw out new ideas. "Tough break," he said at last. "Tough break."

I placed a basket of candy at every place setting, and a noisemaker and a party hat. My hands trembled as I put the silverware down. I wondered how he felt on this celebration of his daughter's birth. Did he remember the original day and his first sight of her in the world?

"So you're at the hospital all the time?"

"Yes." Was it to be an incantation of my days?

"I hate hospitals," Eddie said. "The smell."

"It brings out anxieties," I said.

"No, it's the smell. I've always been sensitive to odors."

"You get used to it."

"Is Jay in pain?"

"Sometimes. His back. He's weak, fatigued."

Eddie sighed and tapped out the now dead ashes from his pipe. "Tough break," he said again.

Then Izzy and the children came in bearing steaming bowls of meat and vegetables and potatoes. We sat down and let the conversation fall to the children, who were elated by the presence of their father at the table. Even Harry and Paul seemed to rejoice. And Eddie was in complete charge, king for a day, carving meat and giving masculine admonitions to all to eat everything and grow strong. He included us in his benevolent gaze as it circled the table. Yet another wife and children. Was there nothing that Eddie couldn't take on? And Izzy, caught in the brilliance of his smile, was radiant and intoxicated. I watched as she put choice food on his plate and passed it back to him in remembered ceremony.

The children blew the noisemakers at each other in earsplitting blasts, and they ate candy recklessly, before they finished their dinner. Then Isabel went to bring in the cake and the oldest child shut the lights. The candles sputtered and cast a pale glow. Janice leaned forward, shut her eyes, and made her wish.

I looked across the table at Eddie and saw that his face was ineffably sad, that he grieved in his own way for the ruins and the losses of decision and chance.

Then Janice blew fiercely at the tiny flames of the candles until they were all extinguished and we sang to her.

16

Insomnia again and why not? The worst fantasy of all had become the truth. I was going to be abandoned. In a sense I had been abandoned already. I rolled over onto my stomach and lay there baby-style, limbs loose. What now? Maybe a complete regression, thumb-sucking and all. Except that I had never really done that. I did other things, disposed of other truths a long time ago, lay in bed rocking and loving my own body. And I was in charge then, could make things be the way I wanted them to be —or else. But not now. The power had been lost somewhere in transit, and I could only go back and remember. Yet it was a comfort, this new nocturnal ritual. Reaching in blindly I pulled out another time when I had been threatened by loss, a time when Jay had been less than perfect. Or had not. It didn't really matter now. But I could still revive the feeling.

We were at a studio party when the name Diana came up in conversation and I was instantly alerted. Someone teased Jay about it—a girl who worked on the show, did continuity or something, a girl with a myopic squint and spittle in the corners of her mouth when she laughed. She said his name in two syllables, "Ja-ay," implying shared knowledge, and she teased him about Diana. I had been to rehearsals and other parties and I had heard the name before. She was one of that lineup of dancers who do all the fancy footwork on the Jerry Mann show, just before Jerry parts the curtains and comes through each week. I didn't know which one she was, might never know. The brassy opening theme played in my head. There were always ten girls, a reasonable variety of blondes and brunettes and two token blacks. They changed and yet they remained constant. One of them was named Diana.

The party continued and I looked at Jay, appraising him, but I didn't detect any change. What did I expect anyway? Guilt inscribed on his forehead? Little furtive glances, a new nervousness in his style? Nothing doing. Jay was himself, having fun, catching my glance instead of evading it. He was a little drunk and his look was sensual, misted and suggestive. I smiled at him, full of terror and response. I looked for clues and there weren't any. All that married ease between us, a thousand messages flashed with the eye, with little body gestures. Jay was having a good time, but he'd be ready to go home in a little while. He'd want to make love after the party and so would I, almost as an extension of the camaraderie between us as we moved separately in that crowded room.

What did she mean, that awful laughing cow of a girl? What was the leering insinuation? Dancers do have a reputation, unfounded or not. They're something like nurses, who will do anything for anyone—that's common knowledge. All that white, those creamy stockings, those starched haloes only a blind for redhot sensuality. Why not dancers too? Look at the suggestion in the choreography of their movements, those practically nonexistent costumes. Why should Jay resist that temptation if it was there all the time? If it was something he was forced to focus on through the prism of the camera lens? Floating overhead on a dolly, getting a new aerial perspective of all that sensual jazz. Dancers *are* beautiful. Even the ones who aren't classically pretty have something. Those legs for one thing, and muscles like little surprises everywhere in delicate frames. Shaven armpits, the shiny perfume of sweat, all that music behind them so that they even *walk* and chew their food with a certain syncopation. I imagined a Diana doing her turns on stage, blackened bare feet, the exotic claims of stage makeup, costume, breathlessness.

Another cameraman was talking about something, the mysteries of a Bergman film, I think. The girl who had spoken about Diana was leaning forward, nodding at him. The cameraman ended every sentence with "Right? Am I right?" It was hard to concentrate. Another conversation to my left overlapped this one, so that everyone was talking gibberish. I wanted to go home, felt a constriction in my chest that was like pain. I sent my signal to Jay, who was on the other side of the room now, at what seemed to be a great distance. He read my message and came slowly toward me with little detours among his friends. I watched as he went into a group and made them laugh, watched friendly pats on the backsides of women, little boxing gestures exchanged with the men. He was still smiling when he came up to me. "Right. You're absolutely right," I said to the cameraman, and then I separated myself from the group to meet Jay. He put his hand on my arm immediately and it struck me again that Jay liked to *touch* all the time, that tactile gesture often took the place of language. With the kids too, his hands always on them, as if he would memorize their bones, circling an ankle or a wrist with his long fingers. Something in me liked it of course, needed it, curled and curved to his touch even in ordinary household conversation.

But now I found myself leaning away. Ah, body language. Jay moved closer, enforcing his hold on my arm, as if to emphasize a point he had just made. I thought my flesh might darken under the still light pressure of his fingers. I expected him to be alarmed, to sense the danger of my suspicion, but he only said, "Ready to go? Had enough?" And I nodded, trying to seem like myself as we worked our way through the room to the door.

I drove home and he played little games with me in the car, whispering endearments into my hair. I could smell the heavy sweetness of his drinking breath. "You know," he said, and I knew the expansiveness of his mood from the slow way he was speaking; "you know," he said again, "you were the prettiest woman at the party, by far. By far," he repeated, as if someone had disputed it. "And do you know what I've been thinking all night?" His hand rested on my knee as if he were going to confide a great and vital secret.

It interfered with my own thoughts. Diana. The two of them in some lovely little routine full of sensual gestures, not a word passing between them. Jay always looked like something of a dancer himself, or like someone about to break into a dance routine, given the moment and the music. Face it, face it. Women always liked Jay. Door opener, listener, package carrier, toucher extraordinaire.

It would have been easy enough to just say it then. Diana! Or, who was that woman I saw you with last night? That was no woman, that was a sweet little dancer in Jerry's stable. You know how they are, dancers. Like nurses, if you know what I mean.

And what if he *had* broken that fierce bargain, and he wasn't faithful? What would it really mean anyway, in terms of what would happen between us? Lying in bed, sleepless, I remembered that conversation a long time ago about fidelity. What would you do if I was like your father? But I couldn't say. You're *not* like him . . . Yet the potential is there, I suppose, in everyone. Izzy had asked me once if I would give Jay life if it were with another woman, if . . . and I had said yes. But that would be an abandonment too, wouldn't it?

I had wondered if she was one of the black girls. God knows they're beautiful now that they know it, allow themselves to be. Jerry always had a partiality for the black girls on the show, for that mask of conviviality they showed him, feeding him soft Southern voices, that drew on the magic of their myth.

"Who's that girl with the thick glasses?" I asked Jay.

"Connie?" He was surprised. I had nudged him away from the direction of lovemaking, and into an ordinary conversation. "She's a good kid, but a little anxious. Everything's passed her by. And she's been in love with Jerry for years."

"Ugh," I said, shuddering.

"Ah," he said. "I expect more compassion from you, Sandy, old kid. Pretty women can afford to be generous to their less fortunate sisters."

"It was *Jerry* I meant with that 'ugh.' "

"Not your type, huh?" He moved closer again, stroked my ear.

"Don't be funny, Jay. And stop *doing* that while I'm driving. Sometimes I don't understand this whole chemistry business anyway. Who wants who. It's not as simple as pretty faces, good legs, is it? I mean Jerry is really *un*attractive when you see him close up."

"Jerry is a star, for God's sake! Stardom transcends reality." He leaned back and hummed the opening bars of Jerry's theme, and in my mind's eye the little chorus moved onstage, kicking their legs skyward, viciously sexy and smooth.

I remembered the dumb-ass conversations I had for years with Izzy and other girls at school about whether we'd care if a man we truly loved went with another woman for, you know, just sex, or would it *really* bother us, if he went for say, intellectual stimulation. Oh God.

I couldn't ask him then. I couldn't say a word. Just let him slide back into the old bedside approach while I parked the car. In the short whining climb of the elevator, he played the bones of my spine (an old, but working trick). Ah, why couldn't I just let it go? WIFE AND MOTHER, the inspiration for a thousand greeting cards, winner take all. It was all based on nothing but the slightest hint anyway, the most subtle of intuitions. Yet something in that girl's voice offered pages of possibilities. If asked, she might have gladly produced documented proof from her purse.

What would you do if I were like your father? I don't know. You couldn't . . .

The baby-sitter paid and dismissed. Jay, good Daddy, going in first to cover the children. "Jesus, they are *beautiful!*" Bursting with his excesses, urging my own. "Come look at these kids, Sandy," as if he had invented them. Come look at this view, that crazy skyline, this terrific food, this beautiful erection. Just for you, darling. His appetites were so huge you could not imagine standing in their way.

On the other hand, it would really be very simple. Face

him in the good old married lamplight of the bedroom. *Uh*-uh. First things first, kiddo. Tell me about Diana.

Who?

Your little Ginger Rogers, Fred. You know who.

Head in hands now, penis dropped from grace against his thigh.

All right. All right. It happened once, Sandy. I swear it. Do you know, I wanted to tell you? Do you remember the Sunday when I was so damn restless I couldn't even read the *Times*? When I sighed all afternoon until you couldn't stand it? The Sunday after the damned rehearsal Jerry wouldn't let go. Egomaniac bastard.

So you choreographed a little fucking?

It happened, Sandy. Wow, how do I expect you to believe that? Of course it didn't just happen. I did it. She did it.

Birds do it, I might sing. Bees do it, for heaven's sake.

Then, Jay would continue, I decided *not* to tell you, because I didn't want to cause you that kind of pain. If you can only believe that now. Because of everything. Your mother and father. Because in the long run it doesn't even matter. It wasn't memorable, Sandy, in any sense of the word.

Just fun while it lasted, huh?

And the keys came out of his pocket and were silenced on the dresser top next to the loose coins. The clothes were thrown everywhere. Slob. Does he think I'm the goddam maid around here?

Then he stretched in that way he always had, loose and reaching. Clock-winding. Covers pulled back. Good-Mother-Father-Jay, fixing the room for love, for sleep. Nothing so domestic with what's her name, I'll bet. All

96

tangled sheets and hot breath there. Or stained car up-
holstery.

"Come here, sweetie," Jay said. Arms opened. "Come
here."

And I walked around the bed, feeling my way like a
blind woman, teetering on my poor reluctant feet. You
can't accuse a man of your own *fantasies*, can you? And
it's possible to become your own mother, isn't it? I didn't
want to know, anyway. That was how imagination became truth. You had to accept it first, allow your will to
be broken.

I let myself be kissed, a passive resister, until a choice
had to be made. And then I kissed back. "Love," Jay
said. "Here," reduced to parts of speech. His hands
worked, redefining my own forms.

"Okay," I said at last, letting her go, ghost dancer,
twinkle-toed homewrecker, figment of a distant and terrible imagination. And I was saved.

17

January 16th

Dear Children,

How are you? We are fine here in the land of palm trees and sunshine. Today our Cultural Discussions Unit is meeting on the beach for a session of Yoga exercise and meditation. So far I have not done well in this area as I am unable to empty my mind of all that junk I carry around with me so that I can concentrate on reaching a higher spiritual state.

When I get into that position with my legs crossed first thing I get a terrible cramp. You know me and my varicose veins. Anyhow I shut my eyes because I can't help it if I look at anybody else I start to laugh. (Shame on me). The leader with some figure she can twist herself up like a pretzel tells us we have to get rid of everything before we begin. Some job my head is always crowded with this and that. She talks with a very serious face about Life Force.

98

We have to breathe in a certain way I get dizzy and in the meantime I am thinking of my shopping list for supper and did I shut the gas and what you are doing so far away in New York.

As far as Sam goes he falls asleep right away and has to quit. Well in any case I feel that the exercise and the fresh air can't hurt anybody and it is better than sitting around moping. In the meantime before I empty my mind again let me remember to send my best regards to your parents Sandy and to my dearest grandchildren.

Love and peace
Mona

18

In the supermarket, Paul sat in the seat and Harry pushed the wagon through the aisles. I walked alongside them, pulling boxes and cans from the shelves, and dropping them into the wagon. I threw weightless boxes of cereal with the words FREE FREE LOOK INSIDE! printed in big letters. After them, I tossed bloody cuts of meat, wrapped and sealed as if they had been readied for a time capsule. I felt a sick sensation in my chest, and I wondered if I might become a vegetarian. I could not even inspect the meat for distribution of fat or bone or gristle. I shut my eyes and then I wiped my hands on the sides of my coat. Every few minutes the children would call out the name of a product they had seen in a television commercial. "Get it," they demanded and, weary of the ordered idiocy of our lives, of the cautions against cavities and unbalanced diets, I complied. "Here," I said, "okay," until Paul's lap was covered with packages and I wasn't even sure of what I had taken.

In the pickle and relish aisle, Mr. and Mrs. Caspar, who lived in our building, walked toward us. He pushed the wagon and she preceded him, slapping the floor in Swedish clogs. Her hair was tortured into a teetering pile of curls, snaked with ribbons and artificial blond braids. She was at least as old as my mother, but she wore a tiny, pleated skirt, and the flesh of her thighs trembled with every step.

Behind her, Mr. Caspar, still handsome, rangy and weathered as an aging cowboy, walked with his head down, pushing the wagon as if it carried an intolerable load. In fact, it was almost empty. Just a loaf of bread and a few other items were at the bottom. Cradled in her arms were the gourmet items: olives stuffed with capers and almonds, smoked oysters, a jar of brandied fruit. Coming abreast of us, Mr. Caspar addressed himself to the children. He took a handkerchief from his pocket and began to change it into wriggling, writhing animal shapes. Paul giggled.

"I lost my penny," Mr. Caspar cried. "I can't find my penny." He pretended to search in his wagon and then in ours. Mrs. Caspar's lips lifted, showing the yellow sides of her teeth, the dark red of her gums. She sighed, trying to catch her reflection in a huge jar of pickles. She poked at her curls.

"My penny, my penny," Mr. Caspar cried. His hand reached out, cupping Harry's ear, and we all heard the clink of a coin against his ring. "Ah," he said.

Harry poked his finger cautiously in his ear.

"Only one," Mr. Caspar said. "I only lost one."

"Me," Paul said.

"Keep your eyes open, Sonny," Mr. Caspar warned. "Maybe next time. How is your husband?" he asked me.

"He's sick," I said.

"Well, if we could help you out sometimes . . ." But it was an editorial "we." Mrs. Caspar had fled the aisle. We could hear the receding noise of her clogs, the jangling of her jewelry.

"Thank you," I called, as he hurried after her.

The whole neighborhood knew about Mrs. Caspar, about Estrella. "Estrella, my foot, if you'll pardon me," said Joseph's mother. "She got that name from a five and dime someplace. And if she only acted her age, she would be in the old ladies' home."

Even my parents knew about her, although Mrs. Caspar didn't patronize their shop. "That's the whore of Babylon," my mother said. A grim statement.

My father smiled indulgently. He spiraled his finger around his ear. "Nuts," he pronounced. "Harmless."

"She roams the streets," my mother insisted.

"Ah, she doesn't do anything. Who would want her? She thinks she's Elizabeth Taylor. She runs around like someone's chasing her." He shook his head and clucked his tongue. "She's a sad case."

"Her husband is sad," I said. "He's always smiling."

"That's sad?"

"No, I mean *always*. A little desperate smile. He looks close to tears."

My mother folded her arms and shrugged. My father smiled. But what they said was common knowledge. Estrella Caspar went out alone at night. Mr. Caspar used to follow her, ducking in the shadows. But she spoke of other men who followed her, who flirted: butchers, taxi drivers, young sailors. She gave beauty and romantic advice freely to younger women in the elevator, in the laundry room. A blond streak, she advised. A darker eyeliner. She hurried from the building, eager to pursue the wonders of the night, and Mr. Caspar, with his sad little smile, a grimace really, waited for her to come home again.

In the supermarket I stalked the aisles, filling the cart until Harry was unable to push it. I looked at the foods that were Jay's favorites: the raisin cookies, tangerines in great golden pyramids, the marshmallows that we used to toast on forks over the gas jets.

Paul called out the name of yet another sugar-coated breakfast cereal.

"That's enough!" I said, in a voice so sharp that it forced his glance down. "You can't fill yourself up on all that junk," I added, trying to sound more reasonable, maternal. But he wouldn't be fooled. He kicked his heels against the cart in an angry tattoo.

At the checkout counter we came up behind Mr. Caspar, unloading his basket. Mrs. Caspar was a few feet away, talking to the store manager, who kept looking up uneasily, smiling and trying to back away. She held him with one long red-tipped finger poised on his sleeve, and with the shrill insistence of her voice.

Paul kicked harder, catching Mr. Caspar in the small of his back. "Don't!" I cried and I grasped his ankle. "I'm sorry," I said to Mr. Caspar, but he had turned, his face already arranged in that same smile. "Where is that other penny?" he asked. "Where did it go?"

Paul, who had been prepared to weep, was caught, his eyes only shining with tears.

"Here it is," Mr. Caspar said triumphantly. He pinched Paul's nose gently and a coin clinked into his palm.

19

Again, that night sleep wouldn't come, and I lay there, eyes opened to the rough white sky of the ceiling, and tried to work *my* magic. But I couldn't evoke Jay this time, couldn't bring the comfort of his presence to that room. I got out of bed and began to pace. If this kept up I would have to take something, ask Dr. Block for some pills to do the trick. You can't depend on the imagination forever. You can't depend on anything. I paced as if I was angry. I *was* angry, stomping across the floor at two in the morning wanting to bellow about injustice and loss. My heart banged in alarm and I was cold.

I went into the kitchen and looked in the refrigerator, an old habit, but nothing offered solace, not milk or jello or fruit. I went to the children's bedroom but once there I closed myself to the innocence of their sleep, to their beauty. So what, I thought. So *what*. I wanted Jay. I wanted him now and for all time. The news had a way of becoming fresh like that. My ears rang, my muscles jerked, as if I had just heard. Jay!

Then, sitting in the stillness of the bedroom again, I thought of his photographs. They always seemed a part of Jay, the way one's voice and language are. I looked through the family album, feeling spent with sorrow. Jay had taken hundreds of pictures of me before Harry was born and at night he had whispered encouragement to the fetus through the stretched skin of my belly. Then he took pictures of the baby himself, born into the world, recording a miracle instead of an ordinary and tragic human event. That was his main quality, the real essence of Jay, his hopefulness, that unswayable pleasure in living. That was why he was willing, even eager to have children, to work at a job he didn't love, to live an ordinary and unpromising life. It was related to the way he touched everyone: me, the kids, his hands making contact with the proof of his convictions. See, it's worth it. It's worth everything.

I closed the album and then I took a large box of prints from a closet, ones that he hadn't had a chance to sort and select from for the book. I carried the box back to bed with me and there was a certain comfort even in its weight on my belly as I settled back against the pillows and opened it.

I felt an immediate sense of relief. It was like finding a responsive face in a roomful of hostile strangers. Jay's sensibility was there in his selection of subjects, and in the mood and composition of the photographs. They seemed both modern and ancient at once. People in tenements or cliff dwellers in lost cities. It didn't really matter. What Jay tried to show was that all change is superficial if the human condition remains the same. He wasn't sentimental either. Elderly people, terrible old ruins, managed to look tough and ironic. There was vanity in the whores and even a certain majesty to their pimps.

But New York City is a bad place to take photographs of people and then just walk away. Everyone is suspicious. Who's that guy anyway, and what does he want? Jay might have been with a finance company or the Narcotics Squad, or even the FBI. It's not paranoid in those streets to believe a stranger is a private detective, a pornographer, a madman. Life is that precarious there, and you can see it in the photographs. Mothers sheltered their children with the wide protection of their arms. "Hey!" they protested to Jay and they cursed him and grabbed for the cameras.

He suffered guilt because of it. He knew that he was an intruder, and yet he felt that it was important, that all the photographs would become evidence in his book, and he would present their case to the world at large. If he asked for permission, it was sometimes given, but then something was lost and the photos became portraits. People posed for him. They clowned, mugged, leered, smiled, crowded into range. "He wants to put me in a book. Hey, I'm gonna be famous! Wait, let me comb my hair, don't show my tooth where it came out. Do I have to smile? Take my sister, she's real cute. Make her famous."

He wanted some of the pictures to be like that, he called them the "personality shots," but he wanted something else too: the unrehearsed face of the community, the sense of a continuing life.

Once he came home with a terrible bruise under his eye.

"What happened?"

"Nothing. Don't get excited. It was just a little scrap."

"A scrap! Do you mean a *fight*, Jay? Do you mean some-

one hit you?" I hovered, nervous and breathless with out-
rage. "Bastards," I said, soaking a cloth in cold water.

"Come on," he said. "Take it easy. It was my own fault
anyway."

"*Your* fault? How could it be your fault?"

"Well, I invade their privacy, don't I? It's kind of a
paternalistic thing I'm doing, isn't it?"

Why did he always take on guilt so easily? Why was
he so damned fair and good? "Shit!" I said. "You're an
artist."

"Thanks for that, anyway," he said, as I laid the wet
cloth against his eye.

It occurred to me now, in this lonely bed, that the key
to everything that had happened was in his goodness.
Goodness=vulnerability=weakness. I'm crazy, I thought,
but some part of me still believed it. Had he been a little
tougher, less *good*, then nothing, not even death would
have challenged him. But he was an open place, just like
his own father. They were felled saints who seemed to
lie down gladly. Then how would I teach my own sons?
To avoid the bogeyman, boys, you have to *be* the bogeyman. Hit back, hit *first*, for God's sake, and go for the
eyes. But maybe the saintliness was in them already, an
insidious genetic strain, and it was too late. I'm crazy, I
thought, I should be locked up. But I felt, in that tough
surviving membrane of my heart, that it was true.

"Jay," I had said then, "I don't want you to get killed
in action. It's not worth that."

"Ahh, it was only a little misunderstanding. A fellow's
mother. She was deaf. You know, she kept smiling and
nodding. A real beauty, a monument. La Chaise couldn't
invent those forms. The son said I took advantage of her."

"But you didn't. It wasn't your fault."

107

"Yeah," he said. "I know. But they're the Indians and I'm the cowboy. Their disadvantage is historical."

"You go into rich neighborhoods too," I said.

"It's not the same, sweetie. There's hardly anybody in the streets there. Doormen, pekingese, fur coats going into taxis."

"But you'll be fair," I insisted. "You'll show both sides of everything."

Jay laughed. "Your loyalty is a thing of beauty, Madam."

"Well," I said, relaxing a little.

"Listen, I was scared too. I thought he was going to go for the cameras."

"Cameras!" I scoffed.

"Never mind. Love me, love my cameras, baby."

"Jay, don't go back there by yourself anymore."

"Sandy . . ."

"I mean it. It could have been worse." I touched his face lightly near the bruise. "I'm scared."

"I'll protect you," Jay said.

"And who's going to protect *you*, kiddo?" I meant from himself, from his vulnerability.

"You," he said. "And Batman and Robin in there." He gestured toward the other bedroom where the children were sleeping.

"Oh ha ha."

"No, I mean it," Jay said. "We'll go out together, like a street gang. We'll get matching jackets with our name on the backs. We'll be the Avengers, okay?" He put his hand on my neck, cleared a space of hair, and bent forward to kiss it.

"Very funny," I said.

But the next week, the children and I did go with him. It made sense. Who would be suspicious of a family, that unit from which most of us are sprung? We walked along the streets with Jay. I pushed Paul in a folding stroller and Harry ran ahead and then loitered, was alternately the lead and the tail of our procession. We might have been tourists dumb enough to have wandered into tough neighborhoods. But they let us alone. Nobody mugged or even taunted us. Hands came out for money and shadows in doorways took surprising forms. I saw all the sadness and all the beauty with Jay's eyes, and with the eye of the camera.

Before we went home again, Jay took a picture of the children and me in front of a graffiti-streaked wall. There's a timelessness to that picture. I seem happy and very young, standing with my hands in my pockets. The children are in a blur of motion near the skirt of my coat and Harry is smiling for once, unaware of the camera. I look like a sane and decent woman. It's the way Jay saw us, the way he knew me. What would I become when his loving perception of me was gone from this life? I took the picture out now and looked at it for reassurance.

20

Izzy said, "I'm tired of being alone. What's so bad about the nuclear family?"

Izzy said, "Sometimes on Sunday I pretend that Eddie still lives here. I think that Eddie pretends too."

Izzy said, "What do we have to lose? It's good just to be touched."

I let her say everything and I didn't answer.

Then she said, "Let's go, Sandy. It's better than staring each other down. Come on, please come with me. Please."

So I sighed in that long series of sighs that had become an integral part of my breathing and I put on my coat and went to the encounter group with her. Somehow I expected something more athletic, a large gymnasium and people with their hands on their hips, waiting for a whistle to be blown. Play ball!

But it was an ordinary room where someone had once lived. Furniture had been removed, but impressions had been left on the faded green carpet and I could imagine where the sofa had been and the tables and chairs. The people seemed to be patients waiting for attention at a free clinic. In the absence of furniture, they slouched and leaned against the walls. There were six men and seven women. Two of the women were twins, somewhere in their forties, dressed identically. They stayed near one another and I could see the remarkable details of their sameness, natural and assumed. They moved the same way and folded their arms and blinked too often. In the left corner of each curling mouth was an applied beauty spot in the shape of a star. I wondered if I would want to touch them. A man squatted at their feet: compact, wiry, with dark curly hair that emerged from the short sleeves of his green polo, from his small simian ears, from the dark tunnels of his nose. What if he touched me? There were two fat people, a man and a woman, with great pendulous rolls of flesh that trembled with every movement, that undulated on their bellies and their breasts. There was one handsome man, a boy actually, wearing sneakers and a mesh tank shirt through which his perfect skin glowed as if it had been oiled. I saw that Isabel was looking at him with deliberate speculation. I remembered dances, adolescent parties, and I almost leaned toward her and said, "He's yours. You can have him."

The group whispered and eyed one another and occasionally a shrill cry of laughter burst from one or another of the twins. I wondered if our leader was among us now, or in some mysterious way would only be an unseen presence or a voice. Perhaps we were being watched and were expected to begin some sort of contact with each other.

But the contact was only visual. An old man looked at me for a long time, and I saw the wasting of his flesh, the comical sag of his trousers, and the loose loop of the collar around his neck. Would I touch that skin?

Izzy poked her elbow against my hip and she smirked. "Don't blame me," she said, out of the side of her mouth.

"If I write to Mona about this, she'll think she wrote to herself."

"It looks like her kind of crowd. *Uh*-oh, foxy grandpa has his eye on you, blondie."

"Thanks a lot," I said, and I thought of Jay. What if he had been able to grow old like that, and his flesh became a loose sack on his body? And what about me?

The first person I touched that night was myself. Furtively, with the offhand expression of a subway masher, I put my hand across my own waist, moved it over the familiar valley and forward toward the slight swelling of my belly. Solid and real and well known to me. I thought of all the new hands on Jay now, of his fragile bones, and the intimacy of those probing fingers. "I don't feel so well," I told Isabel. Just then our leader came into the room.

At least *she* looked athletic. In her black leotards, she resembled a dancing teacher. She was very short and she had no-nonsense close-cropped gray hair. She went slowly across the room, speaking to each person in turn, and shaking hands. The room grew quiet as we strained to listen. But all she said was, "Good evening, I'm happy to meet you. Good evening, I'm glad you could come," as if she were the hostess at a garden party. "How are you?" she said to me, and I found myself bracing my foot against the floor in case I would be thrown off balance. Then she moved to the center of the room. Raising her arms above her head she stretched, exaggerating the movements, yawning. "Oooooh," she said. "That feels good. Why don't you try it? No, come on, I mean *really* try it. Extend yourself, move that elastic body."

The fat woman lifted her arms slightly above her head and made a mewling sound.

"That's right," the leader said. "Give a little and then a little more. Experience that stretch, experience the luxury of it." Then she lay down on the floor and the dark hairy man immediately lay down beside her. A few people snickered. "What's your name?" she demanded. "First name only."

He cleared his throat. "Ahem. Ahem. John. Johnny."

"Oh," she said, rolling away from him. "That's a good name. I want to experience that name. Say it with me, everybody. Roll it around in your mouth. Joh-un, Joh-un-ny. Joh-un."

"Say, that's my name too," the fat man said. "Listen, you can call me Big John," he said. Then he bent over, grunting, took off his shoes, and threw them into a corner.

"Big John," the leader said. "Come here, Big Joh-un."

Big John lay down beside her, smiling slyly at the fat woman, who still stood with her arms folded across her breasts.

"Joh-un-ny," we all chanted. "Big Joh-un."

A dark woman in sunglasses poked me. "What the shit is that supposed to mean?" I shrugged and she said, "I mean, what is it supposed to *mean*?"

Then the leader told us all to take off our shoes and leave them against the wall. "Nobody wants to get hurt," she said. She reached her hand out to one of the twins, who immediately attached herself to her sister, and the two of them joined the group on the floor.

"What the hell," said the woman in sunglasses, and she stretched out on her stomach, kicking her legs in the air.

One by one we all lay down. The last one was the old man and we could hear the terrible snapping of his joints as he lowered himself. "Sidney Farber," he said, from a supine position, extending his hand.

"First names, first names," said the leader.

"Sid," he said. "Call me Sid."

We hissed and writhed like snakes, experiencing Sid's name.

Then the twins demanded to know the leader's name and she said that we were to call her Bunny, and we all chanted, "Burny, Bunny, Bunny."

"That's a soft name," said a twin.

"It's a cuddly name," said the other.

"Ah, but do I feel soft?" Bunny demanded. "Come on, find out." She rolled over onto her stomach and shut her eyes, looking like someone about to receive a rectal thermometer.

Sid crawled stiffly across the floor and touched her arm.

"Leave it to the old ones," Sunglasses said. "The first ones to use their hands."

"But that's what we're here for," said a skinny blonde in velvet dungarees.

"Yeah, well," said Sunglasses, not convinced.

We incanted the names, lying on the floor with our eyes shut, with our eyes open, hands touching down the length of the room. "Sa-an-dy, Si-id, Is-a-bel, Cyn-thi-a, Bi-ig Joh-un."

"Say," said Big John, "how's about we do the one with the rocking back and forth. Remember that one, Pearl?" he said to the fat woman.

Bunny shook her head. "Obviously Big John has been to other sensitivity sessions and wants to do something he remembers."

"So? He's not the leader," Little John said.

"*Bunny* is our leader," pouted a twin.

"And she's soft," said the other.

"God, are they for real?" asked Sunglasses. But no one answered her.

"We all want to feel safe in this room. We all want to feel close to one another. Everybody stand up now," Bunny said. "Stand up and we'll form a circle."

The handsome boy in the mesh shirt hadn't said anything, but he quickly took my hand and we moved into the circle. Isabel gave him a fast tragic look and reached for my other hand. A terribly cross-eyed woman in a flowered dress cut between the twins, who squealed in protest.

"They don't like to be apart, those two," observed Little John.

"Siamese twins," Pearl said, as she stood and pulled her panties out of her crotch. She walked between the other two men, both middle-aged and wearing sweat socks, and took their hands.

"Now shut your eyes," Bunny said. "Shut your eyes and experience the darkness."

"Oh good," Pearl said. "We're going to do 'blind.'"

"Now," continued Bunny, "are you experiencing the darkness?" Someone moaned softly. "Do you feel the density and the blackness and the silence? Do you see, even darkness has a texture."

One of the twins giggled and someone else said, "Shhh."

"Okay," said Bunny. "Now drop hands and choose someone. Quickly. A partner. I'll be someone's partner, too, and we'll come out even."

Sid and Handsome each took one of my hands and Sid looked sad and dropped the one he held. Handsome scratched across the palm with one finger.

"Don't," I said, but he looked blankly ahead and waited for further instructions.

"Now we're going to pretend we're blind, that half of us are blind. We're going to experience the dark world of the blind, the very texture of it. But we're going to feel safe and protected because one partner in each couple will be able to see. The seeing partner is going to lead his 'blind' partner around the room. Everyone will have a chance to be blind. Everyone will have a chance. Put your arm around your partner. Feel his presence."

"Say, that's not my presence," someone hooted. Someone else said, "Be serious. This isn't a game."

It was my turn to be "blind" first and before I shut my eyes I looked around quickly and saw Izzy paired with Little John and the twins clutching one another. Then I shut my eyes and Handsome led me around the room, his hand too high on my waist and then too low on my hip. I hated the darkness. I shut my eyes so tightly that flashes of color broke the blackness. I hated the feel of his hand on my waist, not Jay's hand. I wondered if I would fall, if I would plunge without stopping into some darker place than the one behind my closed lids. I felt relieved when Bunny instructed us to change places. But Handsome cheated, letting a slit of light in through the incredible mesh of his lashes.

"Don't you trust me?" I asked, and I could tell by his faltering step that he had finally shut his eyes.

After everyone had been both "blind" and "leader," we sat on the floor again. "Scramble up," Bunny said. "Sit next to someone else." Izzy drew Handsome and I sat next to Sid, who looked surprised, and smiled.

"Now touch, go ahead and touch, gently now, no genitals please. Experience the texture of the partner: the hair, the skin, the body warmth. Touch and know that you are being touched, that we can reach one another

116

in this simple way. Stroke, if it gives pleasure. Pat and stroke and touch."

The cross-eyed woman looked at her own nose and stroked Big John's leg. "That's wonderful, Sophie," he said. "Sophie, you are wonderful." And Sophie's face opened in a smile.

Sid's hands were as soft as a girl's, and he touched in brief, tentative pats. I touched his arm, and then I moved closer and put my hand across the creepy yellow skin of his neck and I heard a deep sigh of pleasure leak from him like air escaping from a tire.

"Now what are you feeling?" Bunny asked. "Tell us what you are feeling."

"I feel relaxed," the thin blonde said, as Bunny massaged her back in long, slow strokes.

"Cynthia feels relaxed," Bunny said. "Let yourself go limp, Cynthia. Let yourself feel free against the movement of my hands."

"I feel nervous," said one of the twins. Little John paused in stroking her leg.

"No, don't stop," Bunny instructed, and he continued to move his arm in mechanical strokes.

Tears came to the twin's eyes. "I still feel nervous, I can't help it. I don't think we should be here doing these things."

"Why don't you go home then?" Pearl asked.

"Because I like it," the twin said, beginning to weep. Her sister jumped up and put her arms around her.

"Don't stop," Cynthia said to Bunny.

"Sometimes we feel guilt over receiving pleasure," Bunny said, raking across Cynthia's back.

One of the middle-aged men was massaging Sunglasses' feet. "I like it better when I'm done than when I do," she confessed.

"We want to be babies," Bunny said. "We want to be

free of worry and guilt. We want to have things done for us. We want to remember lying on the dressing table. Mother pats the powder here and there, touching secret places, making us quiver. Mother makes sweet cooing sounds and her soft hair tickles our bellies. How does it feel to have Mother doing these things for you?"

"My mother is dead," Little John said.

"John feels sad, remembering his mother is dead."

I tried to remember being a baby, and my mother's hands, but Sid's stroking, monotonous now, abrasive, intruded.

"She died when I was a baby," Little John said. "My aunt brought me up. My father's sister."

"Do you remember how it felt to have your aunt do things for you, John?"

"She was a strict woman. She never touched anybody with a ten-foot pole."

"Poor John," Cynthia cried out. She leaped from her place and ran to him, throwing her arms around his neck.

"Cynthia feels sorry for John. She feels like mothering him."

Big John walked over to Little John. He patted his head. "We're all with you, kid."

"Mother!" Little John cried. "Mother!"

"Take it easy," Pearl said, and she pulled his head onto her mountainous bosom.

"Mother!" he cried again, but his voice was muffled.

I looked across the room and saw that Izzy was lying back against Handsome's chest, and that he was playing the nipple of her left breast as if it were a guitar string. Her eyes were shut.

"Come on everybody," Bunny said. "Let's show John that we care about him. Let's give him our support." We crowded around John, who had worked himself into a breast-beating frenzy.

"We love you, John." "Take it easy, fella." "You're our boy, Johnny."

Then Pearl pulled away, letting his head drop with a dull thud to the carpet. "I think that's enough," she said. "I hate to say this, but I think that John is selfish."

Cynthia stood on her knees. "You only want to call attention to yourself."

"Who, me?" Pearl asked. *Me?*

"You!" the twins said in chorus. Then one of them continued. "You're an absolute slob. You and fat man have been trying to take over all night."

"Do you feel threatened?" Pearl shrieked, and the twins cowered.

"Why do you feel it necessary to resort to name-calling?" Bunny asked.

"Because they make me angry."

"So you feel angry. Does your sister feel angry too?"

"Yes," one of them said. "We always feel the same things. It's a psychic phenomenon."

"Bullshit!" Sunglasses said. "What a load of bullshit!"

"Mother," Little John moaned, but no one listened.

"You have no right to attack my physical appearance, you little runt. This happens to be a thyroid condition."

"Bullshit, bullshit."

Sophie ran into the center of the room and waved her arms for silence. "Why don't you attack me?" she asked. "Why don't you pick on my poor eyes?"

"Nobody is even *talking* to you!" Pearl shouted.

I looked around the room and saw that Handsome and Izzy were locked in an embrace. Poor Izzy, I thought. But then there was poor aging Sid, and poor motherless John, and poor Pearl. We were all such dreadful and pitiable creatures of this life that I wanted to throw back my head and let out an earth-splitting howl. I pushed Sid's hands away and opened my mouth, but it was Bunny's voice that I heard.

"Believe it or not—now hold it everybody, just for a second!—believe it or not, you're touching. Now! With your voices, with your anger. Let the anger out. Let's be animals and let the animal rage loose. On all fours, now! Growl! Roar! Let it out!"

We prowled the room on our hands and knees, and I kept thinking at least this is making me tired, and later I'll be able to sleep.

"OWOOO!" The other animals circled me and grew tired too, until one by one we lay silent in a chaotic pattern on the floor. The green carpet was musty and rough against my cheek, but I pretended that it was grass, and that Jay was beside me in some early beginning place.

21

My cold was getting better. On Sunday, the last day of my exile from the hospital, I took the boys to the beauty shop for haircuts. My parents made the usual joyous fuss over them, commenting on their size although they had seen them only three days before, on their beauty, on the bliss they created simply by being. My father actually called Harry "Champ" and sparred with him, and Harry laughed and shut his eyes against the loving blows. I saw that my father was trying to be the masculine presence for my children in the absence of *their* father, and I was touched. I knew that in the future he would throw footballs and baseballs to them with the changing of the seasons, and ruffle their hair and speak to them in grave, deep tones.

The boys spun on the chairs as I had done as a child and looked solemnly back at the reflection of their faces rising from the pink capes as my father cut their hair.

My mother, not in uniform now, walked around the

shop and out of habit rearranged jars and bottles and opened drawers and shut them. "Sweetness!" "Dollface!" she cried alternately to the children and pinched their cheeks and caught them with kisses. When their hair lay in wet, final grooves and their smells were flower sweet, she gave them money. Their fists overflowed with coins.

"They don't need money," I said.

But I was overruled. "Let them buy something," she said.

"What are you going to buy, Champ?" my father asked.

"Let them buy toys. Let them buy candy." They were spilling out their love in frantic lavish drifts and it made me feel sad.

On the way home we stopped at the playground, even though it was a very cold day with a stinging wind. There were only three or four other children there, neglected children perhaps, or ones with crazy mothers like myself. They moved aimlessly, like bums, from one thing to another, sifted darkened sand in the sandbox, hung listlessly from the swings, and eyed one another as potential enemies. There is something dangerous about days like this, I thought. The wind was bitter and there were tears in my eyes that did not come from the grief hoarded and hidden somewhere below.

Another woman came into the playground, and it was as if I had willed her there for distraction or companionship. She was overweight and cozily sloppy, with wildly windblown hair and what appeared to be house slippers on her feet. She was looking for her dog. A leather leash dangled from one hand and she whistled repeatedly, a rising, questioning sound. Then she walked to the bench where I was sitting and she smiled at me. "That dog's going to drive me nuts," she said.

I nodded.

"Ninety bucks on training," she said. "Forty bucks on shots. Fifteen on *grooming*."

"I know."

"Then he takes off like a bat out of hell. Males. I'll never get another one, if you know what I mean."

I nodded again and she was encouraged. She sat down next to me. "Those your kids?"

"Yes," I said, too weary to explain that just two of them were mine.

She whistled again, softly. "Some gang, God love them. No wonder you keep them out on a day like this. They must drive you up a wall." She squinted at me, speculating. "You *look* tired."

"Well," I said. "My husband is very sick."

"Ohhhhh. So you want to keep them out of his hair, huh?"

"No, no, he's in the hospital."

"Serious, huh?" She leaned close to me, so that I could feel her coat sleeve against my own.

"Serious," I repeated. "He's dying."

She moved away slightly as if I had startled or offended her. Her head was cocked to one side. "Doctors don't know everything," she said. She stood and cupped her hands to her mouth. "Rusty! Rusty!" she bellowed, and then she sat down again. "Maybe I'd be better off if he never came back," she confided.

"He has cancer," I said, unrelenting.

"That so?"

"He's thirty-two years old." I stared at her, pressuring her for a response. Why shouldn't she know? I wanted her to know.

But she was crafty, evading my evil eye. *"My* husband doesn't believe in doctors," she said. "He says they're all crooks. Hocus-pocus. And who do you think pays for all those fancy offices? For those nice leather couches and all? And those vacations they take! Do you think there's a doctor in New York on a day like this? No, they're smart. They're in Florida, in Arizona. They're out on the golf course, taking life easy. On *your* money," she added, pointing an accusing finger.

"He's dying." I said again, believing it myself in a terrifying swell of knowledge. I wanted to shake that woman until she said yes, acknowledged the truth about Jay, about me, about herself.

But she moved farther away on the bench, her face closed against me. "Even vets," she said. "Fifteen bucks every time that lousy dog gets a sniffle. Do I have to pay for his wife's fur coat?" Her voice was shrill and plaintive with all the unsaid words. Is it *my* fault? What do I have to do with death?

I had an urge to hit her, to punch her in the face, as if the infliction of pain would be the first step in the right direction. But rage and pity rose up in conflict. Poor stupid woman, plump as a bird in her brown winter coat, the leash coiled in her lap.

I stood. "There's your dog," I said, pointing into the distance past the playground.

She jumped up, shading her eyes. "Where? I don't see him."

"There," I said. "He's just turned the corner."

She was willing to be convinced. "A big fellow, black?"

"Yes, yes," I said, wanting her to be gone, feeling the tears frozen in their tracks on my cheeks. She went off finally, whistling again, and I called to the boys, telling them it was time to go home.

In the apartment Paul dropped his coins carelessly on the first surface he encountered, but Harry buried his as proper treasure in the bottom of the toy box.

I lay down on the bed and listened to dance music on the radio. From the apartment next door, I could hear sporadic bumping noises of life. I hummed along with the tune on the radio and then I thought about tomorrow and I wondered if Jay would look different after the few days we had been apart. When would we finally look directly at one another in affirmation of the terrible truth? And what would we say?

Harry came in and watched me from the doorway. I jumped from the bed and swept him into my arms and began to dance around the room with him. He made himself rigid, throwing back his head and howling in what might have been either pleasure or despair.

Hearing the noise, Paul rushed into the room and began to cry, "Me! Do it to me!" He hung on to my legs, dragging his weight.

We danced and whirled and lurched around the room to some innocent bubbling tune of the fifties, until I was exhausted and we fell onto the bed in a warm tangle of the children's arms and legs. "What's going to happen?" I said. "What's going to happen?" Nobody answered.

22

Francis said, "I wondered what happened to you."

"I had a cold. I haven't been here for a few days."

"Well, I'm only passing through now myself. I'm on my way home."

If he was going home, why didn't he leave then? But he was a man in no hurry, open to any possibilities. I was afraid that if he spoke any longer, I might learn something about him, that he would reveal his history and his pathos to me. Yet I stood there with my hand poised on the lucite handle of the hospital door. With a single gesture I could let myself inside and leave him on the other side of the thick glass. And yet I waited, delaying the confrontation with the odors that frightened Eddie, with the rat's maze of corridors, and finally with Jay.

"A cold is dangerous in Jay's condition," I said.

"It must have been hard to stay away."

"Yes." My hand curled over the handle. "I don't know if he's changed."

"Try not to be afraid. He'll see it in your face."

"Do you see it?"

He studied me carefully. He smiled and put a hand on my shoulder. "I see a lovely face," he said.

Blood rushed through the dusty chambers of my heart. "Don't say that."

"I'm only telling the truth," he said.

My hand squeezed the handle of the door and pulled. "I have to go now."

"Don't forget," he said.

In the elevator, climbing to Jay's floor, I wondered what he meant, what it was he wanted me to remember. Then I was there again in that familiar place, with my heels clicking a cadence as I walked toward Jay's room. Practicing in my head the smile that I would use and the way my eyes would look and the words hello hello hello darling hello. With the click-click of my heels I went past the other rooms and they looked out at me with a dull lack of interest, while I thought hello hello hello . . .

Then I was in the room and he was not the same. Would never be the same. So yellow, so thin in just a few days. His ears were large, larger than I remembered them, as if they had grown to accommodate all the sounds he would have to gather and hoard for all time.

"Hello, darling." My voice. "Hello, Martin." How odd that we remember language and the proper words for all occasions. There was no end to my words. I told Jay about Atlantic City and he laughed because I made him think that it was funny. I told him about the funny fat woman on the bus and the nutty old woman at the hotel and the man's suitcase in the bus station. I clowned and rolled my eyes. I imitated everyone's voice and I was surprised at my uncanny knack for doing it.

Martin giggled and said that I should have taken pictures. He had never been to the beach in the winter. It was one of the things he was going to do.

I saw that Jay squinted now, as if he were trying to remember something, and that his hand went again and again to his back.

"Legerdemain, sonny. That's big for magic. Oh God." I wiped my eyes with a tissue.

Jay said, "I wish I had been there with you," and I stopped laughing and looked hard and mercilessly into his eyes. That was the first step.

Then Martin's parents came to visit and they brought his grandmother, who was dramatically old and tiny. "Look who's here," his father said in that harsh voice, and he propelled the old woman toward the chair next to Martin's bed.

Martin was embarrassed and pleased at the same time. He kissed his grandmother's cheek and I imagined the thin papery taste. She could hardly be heard, her voice now worn away to the whining thread of sound on an ancient phonograph record.

Martin's father spoke for her. "Grandma came all the way from the Bronx," he announced.

Her head, her hand, moved in spastic leaps.

And then we all spoke in loud voices. "Isn't that wonderful?" "Isn't she something?"

But I saw that Martin's mother was looking speculatively at Jay and that she observed the changes in him that I observed. Her mouth closed in a narrow white line over her teeth.

I moved closer to Jay in a defensive gesture and I kept my eyes on the incredible labyrinth of lines and wrinkles on the old woman's face. To grow to such a great age, to stay past function and past ecstacy.

Then Jay took some pictures of her and she leaned

forward and removed her spectacles in a final gesture of vanity. In a little while the soft bell rang for the dismissal of visitors. Martin's father lifted his mother from the chair.

"Jay," I said, in a voice that boomed in my own ears, "I love you. Good night, darling."

Even the old woman turned her head at the doorway and looked back.

23

When no one else could do it, Mr. Casper agreed to baby-sit in the evening. "The magic man is here," Paul announced, and a real smile opened on Mr. Casper's face. Our apartment faces the front of the building and his the rear, where the view is of a courtyard and another identical building. I imagined that he would wait later in the dark of my living room, looking through the window for Estrella's return from her night prowl.

I went on my known path to the hospital and discovered that the nursing staff was nervous and expectant. Jerry Mann, the star of the television show for which Jay had been a cameraman, was on his way up. Word had already come from the lobby and there were whispers of excitement and heads poking through doorways all along the floor.

"Jerry's coming," I told Jay.

Martin's parents, hearing the news, paced restlessly in the room. "Him?" rasped Martin's father. "He's terrific.

We always watch him. Don't we always watch him?" He turned to his wife for confirmation.

She nodded. "Do you have your camera ready, Martin?"

Martin's father murmured, as if to himself, "We've watched him for years."

Then the noise of activity grew in the hall, with a few hushing sounds, useless, perfunctory. We heard footsteps and then Jerry was there, big as life, in the doorway. Martin's father seemed stunned for a moment. Did Jerry look so different out of the magic box? Of course. He was human now, with real skin color and pores. He had new dimension and a voice that didn't sound familiar as it adjusted to a pitch and tone appropriate to that room. His wife was behind him and it seemed that she would save the day because she was exotic beyond belief: furred, bejeweled, theatrical. Her voice was some sort of nasal music, touched with a foreign quality I could not place. In the open doorway, faces appeared: awed, happy, some topped by peaked nurse's caps. An elderly patient released her hold on a walker for one treacherous moment, clutched her bathrobe to her throat with one hand and waved with the other. From the corridor, "It's him! Yes, yes, it's him!"

Finally, happy to be useful, Martin's father smiled triumphantly and went to the door and shut it. When we were enclosed in that room, Jerry posed for Martin's camera, with his wife, with Martin's parents. The mother protested for a while, primping her hair, shredding a tissue, and then turned and spoke the very moment the shutter was opened.

Jerry called Jay "Boy." "How are you, Boy?" "We all miss you, Boy." He wasn't a bad actor. He waited for Jay to answer, kept his own expression constant. Would he call me "Girl"? But he didn't. I had met him a few times, with this wife, and the wife before this one, at studio parties, and he remembered my name.

"I watch you all the time," Martin's father said. His voice seemed to startle Jerry's wife, who blinked at him. Jerry gave autographs. For want of something else, he scribbled on a piece of paper that stated THIS PATIENT IS NOT TO BE FED ANY SOLIDS THIS MORNING. He wrote *Yours faithfully, Jerry Mann,* in big impressive script. His wife's perfume and the fragrance of their fame seemed extraordinary in that clinical room. With the door closed he became restless, and looked toward it with furtive but longing glances. The news of the studio ran out quickly. So-and-so is in Spain, is getting married, divorced, transferred. We sat in a dead, nervous silence that forced us to observe everything in the room: the beds, the coiling equipment, the bed charts that listed everything, even the maiden name of each patient's mother. Into the silence Martin's father cleared his throat with a sound of tire chains trying to grip an icy road. Then a few of us spoke at once. "Mr. Mann . . ." began Martin. "Well, I . . ." said his mother.

We laughed and then Jerry told a funny story made even better by its intimate references to famous people. Martin's father laughed and sputtered and choked and his wife had to slap his back. "For heaven's sake," she said. "He loves you on the TV too."

We could hear the visitors' bell chiming in the hall. "Five minutes," called the nurse. "Five minutes."

Jerry stood up first. His hand came out and grasped Jay's. "Okay, Boy. You have to get well now. They're shooting my bad nostril. You hear?" He was perspiring and his face was pale. His wife arranged her fur around her shoulders and he looked at her with an urgent expression.

"Good night, all," she piped through her nose.

Jay thanked them for coming. Jerry kissed me and his flesh was damp and chilled. "Do you need a ride?" I shook my head and he said, "Take care," and grasping his wife's elbow, he steered her toward the door, as Martin's father rushed to reopen it. Good-bye Good-bye. They waved to him and called after him as if he were leaving on a long voyage and would not be seen again on the same channel at the same time on the very next night.

I had become terribly aware of the car now as something large and hulking and patient waiting for me in the parking lot of the hospital. The vehicle that took me to Jay, that took me home again. I could hear the sound of its engine in traffic with the talent of a new mother who hears her own baby in the chorus of squalls from the nursery. It was a particular car, ours, with scars and odors and idiosyncrasies that humanized it.

Old friend, I thought, as I closed the door, encapsulated against the night. But then, riding home, I stopped for a traffic light on a street as empty and still as a Sunday street in a Hopper painting, and the engine moaned and coughed and was silent. A small red warning light on the dashboard glowed and went out. The radio stopped, and the heater. I waited, half expecting that the car would begin again of its own accord. Then I shifted to neutral and pressed the gas pedal tentatively. Silence. This time I pressed more urgently, pumping my foot, thinking vague thoughts about flooding the engine, remembering words like carburetor and points and spark plugs, words heard from the passenger seat as Jay and a mechanic stood and talked in sunlight, patting the hood from time to time as if it were the flank of a beloved horse. I was not even sure if I could lift the hood (was there some intricate catch?) and would I know simply by looking if something had disconnected or burned or worn away? I stepped out into the starry winter night and looked at the car, hunched and quiet, containing its mysteries. I kicked at a tire and rapped my knuckles on the roof.

There were a few stores on the street, serving the immediate neighborhood, and they were closed and dark. There were several houses, but only three had lights visible behind the drawn shades. I would have to knock on one of the doors and explain what had happened. I would ask to use the telephone to call for service on the car, and a taxi to take me home. Yet I didn't, stopped somehow by the idea of disturbing the privacy of those homes, where families were involved in the simple and yet complex business of their lives. Taking baths or reading the newspaper, eating leftovers with their fingers from plastic containers in the refrigerator. I imagined children doing homework in kitchen light and someone laying out the cards for a game of solitaire.

In the distance I could hear the motors of other cars. Perhaps someone would drive down that particular street and see me, and offer to help. "Help," I said softly, and the word dissolved in the air with the vapor of my breath.

What if someone dangerous came along? Boys, for instance, who would seem very nice at first, even deferential. Boys with pretty faces and cold leather jackets. "Can we help you, Ma'am?" Then slowly, in some tribal dance, they would surround me, chanting something in the new language of the streets. I wouldn't know that I was threatened, even laughing at first—"Say, what's going on?" Then knowing that it was hopeless, hearing the end of things in the soft thud of blows to the head, in the sounds of flesh tearing in the name of sex. "Help, help," only whispered now, and terrible clots of blood, tasting strangely like tears in the throat, and darkness and darkness and a new silence.

But it might be Francis, in his blue station wagon with empty cookie boxes on the seat, and a child's shoe beneath it. Francis, shutting the motor off and opening the door like an invitation. "Well come on. Get in. Isn't it lucky I just happened to be riding down this street? I've been thinking about you and your destiny and your loneliness and your husband and the soft pink nipples under that brown sweater. Now just get in and I'll take you home or somewhere without lamplight and I'll give you what you *really* need, never mind that metaphysical crap of spiritual love and loss. What you need, baby . . ."

Click, click, I would start to run along the street. His engine starting again with an explosive snort and the car alongside me with the door still swinging open.

"Get in."

Me running in the slow-motion leaps and bounds of a dreamer.

"You whore. You teasing bitch." The car, pacing me, a manager cruising alongside his panting fighter. "Are you getting in?"

But I would be exhilarated from running, from the transfusion of air, and I would begin to laugh, puffing and laughing at once, and the door of the car would bang shut and I would be left there, laughing and gasping in a cloud of exhaust fumes.

But I sober up fast, walk sedately now, because there is a vintage car, rounded and high, coming down the street. My father toots the horn at me, a playful honk (the way he honks at all the girls—no *harm* in it). My mother is sitting beside him and they are slimmer and very young with no ideas in their heads of ever growing older. My father toots a tune on the car's horn: shave and a haircut—two bits! That's appropriate. My mother slaps his arm and leans out the window. "Come home now, tootsie. It's time for dinner and I'll make something good with steam rising from it and the smell of butter and you can have your old room again and be our pride and joy."

I stop and look inside that car, at the plaid seat covers and the dark polished gleam of my father's hair. I don't know if I want to go inside again, to go back and back and back. In a way it seems more terrifying than going ahead.

Then I don't have to decide because another car is coming and the driver is Jay, and I think, thank God that everything is all right now, that all the horrors are only the dream and all the pleasures are the reality. Because Jay is ruddy and almost round-faced, and his hand is on the steering wheel and he's laughing. He's waiting for me, full of new seed and beauty, and tears come to my eyes because I'm so happy.

"Guess what, I had the most terrible dream. I can't shake it and the essence lingers, but I can see that you're all right and even immortal and we can go home together with your hand resting between my legs and I'll keep touching you and looking at you because I can't shake off this dream. It seemed so real, but I can't tell you the details, they're too painful. Well, all right, Jay. You were sick, oh, I won't even use that word, you know what everybody fears, and it was such a long dream, made up of all the years of my life, it seemed. It was so real, with blood and bad smells and death rubbing its hands together like something in a monster movie. Jay, I'm so happy, I'm so happy."

I began to weep, looking into the window of a shoe repair shop at a pair of nylon lifts for ladies' shoes. I tried to read all the signs: While U Wait, Professional Work,

We Fill Orthopedic Prescriptions. But then my head filled with Jay, and I cried and cried, the only sound on that quiet street.

Then a car came along, scanning the road with its headlights. It slowed as it drew alongside me and the window was rolled down. A woman said, "What's the matter, are you broken down?"

I blew my nose and wiped my eyes before I walked closer. "Yes. I didn't know what to do. I was just getting up the nerve to ask someone if I could use a telephone."

There were several people in the car. The driver, a fat man with a tuxedo on under his overcoat, came out and lifted the hood of my car. "Battery?" he asked. I shrugged and he said, "Did she go on you suddenlike, or flicker out slow?"

"Suddenly." Thinking, mercilessly, without friendship or loyalty.

"Got service?"

I nodded again.

He clucked, felt around under the hood, muttered. "Might be the hose here." Then he closed the hood with a decisive slam. "Okay, we'll leave a flare out here and take you someplace to make a call. Then we can drive you home."

I told him that I didn't live too far away, that I would call from home and just leave the key under the floor mat.

The car was so crowded that I hesitated, but a chorus of voices urged me in. "Come on. There's always room for one more." "Ooooh, you must be freezing!" "Move over, Roseanne. Vincent, sit on Auntie Grace." There was a great shifting and rearranging and suddenly a space opened for me in the back seat. There was a powerful odor of flowers in the car.

"Do you smell the flowers?" asked the woman in the

front seat. She held up an overflowing basket. "We're just now coming from my niece's wedding reception. What a time we had. Wasn't it terrific, Vinnie?" she asked the driver, who had come back into the car again.

"Some party," he agreed.

"This is my husband," the woman said. "These two are my kids. That's my sister-in-law back there with you, and her husband. This is my aunt."

"How do you do?" I said, and the children looked at me shyly and giggled.

"I'll tell you the truth," the sister-in-law said. "I ate myself sick. Such food. You should have seen the Viennese table. It's almost a sin." She sighed happily.

"We'll all see it on your waistline," her husband said, and she jabbed absently at the side of his head. "Look who's talking."

It was warm inside the car. All that body heat, all that easy conversation. Life seemed so reasonable again, so sane.

"What a bride," the old aunt said, in a deep voice. "She was like a movie star. The groom was very good-looking. Tall, long hair like the kids wear."

"A sexy kid," said the woman in the front seat. "They really were a sexy couple."

The old aunt laughed. "Today everything is sex."

I laughed too, shutting my eyes.

"The bridesmaids wore pink, old-fashioned with big hats, you know, and roses. The color scheme was pink and white. Pink tablecloths, pink and white striped candles."

"The way they do things today," the aunt said.

Their voices droned on and on all the way home and I became a part of it, the lighthearted banter, the leftover joy. Then we came to my apartment house. I thanked them all. They shifted in their seats to shake hands and to wave good-bye. "Thank you, thank you," I said. Then I opened the door and was expelled into the world again.

I looked up at the window of our apartment and I thought that I saw a shadow move slowly behind the curtains. Caspar on his night watch. But when I went upstairs and opened the door, I found him sitting at the kitchen table, contemplating his hands. "Hello," I called out. "I'm home."

That smile again. He rose from the chair quickly with an old-world gesture, almost a bow.

At the same time, I raised my hand. "No, don't get up, please. We'll have some coffee."

But he moved to the stove where a pot of coffee was already waiting.

"How nice of you!" I reached into the cupboard for the mugs and brought them to the table. "I'm sorry that I'm so late. Car trouble. I had to leave it somewhere between here and the hospital. I'd better call the garage."

The look on his face changed to one of concern. "But how . . . ?"

"Easy," I said, gesturing with my thumb. "I rode home in style with a wedding party."

He was satisfied then. I telephoned the automobile service and told them the location of the car. Then we sat down and faced one another, hiding our eyes in the steam of the coffee. "Milk? Sugar?"

Silence. All these new dead moments in my life. Throat-clearing, ahem, ahem. Smile. Sip. Silence. "Jerry Mann showed up at the hospital tonight."

"You mean the star? From the big show?"

"The same. He was the hit of the century. The blind could see again. The lame threw away their crutches."

He didn't know what to make of me. His head tilted to one side, the way a dog's does when he expects a command.

"Listen, he's really very nice. It was nice of him to come. Wow, I don't even know what I'm saying."

"Of course. The trouble."

"Yes."

"You're very brave."

Not me, I thought. *I'm* going to live. And live. I sighed, nervous under his paternal gaze. His goodness seemed insufferable.

"So," I said. "It's very cold out."

"I know. I could hear that wind. I had to cover the little one twice."

"Yeah. He fights the blankets off as if they were enemies."

"He talks in his sleep. Sounds only. I couldn't understand the words."

"He finishes the day's work. Settles battles and restores himself as the hero."

"Like everyone does in his dreams," he said.

"I don't dream anymore. I can only sleep a little while at a time. Like a sentry on duty."

"You should take something."

I nodded.

"Me too," he said. "I stay up too. Sometimes the whole night. I hear the children next door wake up and I realize that I haven't slept."

I wondered what time Estrella came home. Did he have a pot of coffee waiting for her as well? Now, whenever I was awake in the middle of the night, I would imagine Mr. Casper awake at the same time, looking out at the empty courtyard, listening for the hum of the elevator.

"Listen," I said. "You were very good to stay with the

140

boys. I appreciate it and they really love you." Like a grandfather, I almost said, but stopped myself.

He waved away my thanks. "I should thank *you*," he said. "Because you know sometimes I'm very lonely."

I waited.

"My wife is a sick woman."

"Yes."

"I know that she's the joke of the neighborhood. But she doesn't even know it. She turns everything into admiration."

How lucky she was to be crazy. To indulge in the luxury of delusion. Some of the dying do that in the hospital. They call out to loved ones who died long ago. The oldest men weep for their mothers again and imagine they are being comforted and cradled. "I'm sorry," I said.

"Thank you." His face was solemn, a sweet release from that smile. A handsome gentle man. "I only hope that she's safe," he said. "I used to follow her, but she's clever and she would elude me. Once I was stopped by the police and questioned."

"Oh God."

"They thought I was something . . . I don't know. Maybe a mugger."

"Not you!"

He laughed. "They come in all types today. I only hope she's safe."

I wondered if he meant that he wished that she were *not* safe, that she would die somewhere away from him. That once and for all he would be done with it. Madness is even worse than dying for the watchers. In his dreams, where he was the hero, was there a great rage in him that shook the earth?

I refilled the cups. Mr. Caspar picked up a deck of

cards that were lying on the counter and began to shuffle them.

"If you're not tired," I said, "would you like to play a game of something? I'm wide-awake."

"Yes, I would like to very much, but I'm not such a great player. You'll have to be patient. Could I just use your telephone first?" I nodded and he dialed and waited and hung up.

"You'll hear the elevator," I said. "And then you can check again."

He shuffled the cards once more and asked what I would like to play.

I shrugged. "Anything. I don't know. I'm not exactly a sharp myself. Jay doesn't play cards. When I was a child my father played Casino with me, or Stealing The Old Man's Bundle. I always won. He would see to that."

"Well, maybe you will always win."

I laughed. "No, it's all right. Honestly, I'm a better sport now. I've built up a tolerance to losing."

"Casino then," he said, starting to deal the cards.

We played a full game. Twice we heard the elevator and Mr. Caspar called his apartment and then sat down again.

While we played, I remembered the kitchen of a place we lived in years ago. My father faced me across the table, and my mother sat somewhere near us, sewing or writing into the accounts ledger for the shop. The table had a swirling pattern of blue and green enamel and it reminded me of paintings I had seen of the ocean. While my father dealt (that was always his job), I ran my hands as if they were ships tilting across the expanse between us. "Pay attention," he would say. "This time I'm going to get you. I feel a lucky streak coming on."

I would stand up suddenly, the joy of winning pushing

me erect. My father held up my hand. "The winner! The world's champion!"

At the end of our game Mr. Caspar had won. "Bravo," I said.

"Only luck. We can have a rematch someday." The elevator could be heard moving past the floor. "Excuse me," he said, going to the telephone. This time I could hear the ringing end abruptly and a thin voice speak to him.

"Ah," he said. "So you're home. Good. I was baby-sitting and I'll be right there."

"She really doesn't mean any harm," he said to me after he hung up. "It's very cold and she came home early."

So, I thought, not quite mad enough to stay out in the cold, to be found frozen in half-light like some bright and fallen bird.

"Good night." A small bowing motion at the door.

"Good night. Sleep well," I said, touching his arm.

24

There were pills for the sleeplessness now, but I didn't want to take them, even though dear Mr. Caspar had advised it. You should take something. My mother called and advised exercise, open windows, vitamins, warm milk. After all, one has to rest.

The pills were in the drawer of the table next to the bed. One at bedtime when needed. Red gelatinous capsules of sleep. I imagined them dissolving and blanketing light, saw sleep itself as the deep red comfort of their color, and was tempted. But there was still the other way. Things to think about, to recall like unfinished business. I tried Jay's side of the bed now, a new trick to bring him closer. Only yesterday I had worn one of his shirts for a while, hoping it would bring an experience of the flesh. But it was only a shirt, faithless, falling to the contours of my own body.

I tried to bring Jay to the room again as I lay in his place, but he was restless and evasive. Here, I said. Over here. Willing him to the bed, moving over slightly and making room for him. But I could only bring him to the window, looking out, and with his back turned to me. We were in the middle of an argument which went something like this:

"Keep your voice down," Jay was saying, thinking of the neighbors, of the children in the next room.

But my voice was my best weapon, sharp and deadly. "I'm not going to baby Harry," I said. "He has to learn to deal with life, just like everyone else."

"For God's sake, Sandy, he *is* a baby! What's the matter with you?"

"There's nothing the matter with me," I said. "There's nothing the matter with wanting your own child to know what's what. He can't just do as he pleases all his life, can he?"

"Sandy, there's only one way to get to a kid, and that's with love. You know that."

"I love him," I said evenly, knowing how cold the words sounded, said that way.

"I know you do." He came to the bed at last, and sat down. "But it doesn't matter if he eats his dinner or not. What matters is what he thinks we feel about him."

I crossed my arms, resisting his gentle flow of logic. "I'm his mother," I said, "and he has to eat. He needs nutrition, doesn't he?"

"Leave him alone for a while. He'll come around." Touching again, playing with one of the places where my arms were joined.

I shrugged him off. "And he has to learn to put things away," I said. "And he's cruel to the baby sometimes. He twisted his foot today when he thought I wasn't looking. And the baby cried."

"Oh come *on,* all kids hate the new baby, Sandy. He wouldn't be normal if he didn't."

"Boy, you know everything, don't you?" The tears were readied behind my eyes. I knew that he was right, of course. Right and wrong. Good and bad. Black and white. I hated the sharp division of things. I knew with a sense of horror that I only wanted to *win,* with Jay, with Harry, maybe even with the infant Paul. To exercise my will over theirs. That little contained streak of cruelty in me threatened to break free. I had shaken a small child because he would not finish his meat, his carrots, his buttered bread. Jesus. How could Jay understand this if he had never witnessed rage in his own childhood? I thought how difficult it was, how impossible all marriages really are, each person coming to battle with separate and complicated histories. It made a case for incest.

But I *was* wrong, and I wanted to be different. Why else did I feel so tearful and full of remorse? I would say it, given the right opening. I'm sorry. Tomorrow I'll be a different woman, reasonable and fair.

Yet I said nothing. I watched as Jay left the room and went in to cover the children. I listened for his footsteps, feeling strangely jealous of my own children, who could be loved simply for themselves, for their very existence. It struck me that this was what Harry felt about Paul, this was his impotence and his rage. The knowledge of shared love, like half-chewed carrots, cannot, will not go down.

When Jay came back to bed, I tried to let him know without language that I was sorry, that I regretted past and future transgressions. I hung on the frame of his back and pressed myself against him. I'll be better now, watch me. You'll see. Until he turned around to face me, pulling me closer, taking me at my word.

25

"He looks terrible," I said.

Dr. Block frowned.

"What about the medication?" I asked. "What about hope?" I thought that I sounded merely petulant.

"I told you," Dr. Block said. "We don't know many things." He coughed into his fist.

I studied him for a while, found nothing hidden, and then I looked around the office, saw diplomas, pictures of his children, of a brown poodle, of a young man (Dr. Block himself?) in a naval uniform.

Then I had the idea. I might have shouted Eureka! in that moment of discovery. I would take Jay home again. In the house he would grow well, nourished by what was dear and familiar. He would awaken at night and see remembered shadows cast by the friendly shapes of our furniture, and fall back into a deep and healing sleep.

How could anyone recover in a place like this, a place that fostered illness, that negated life with its sterile surroundings, its relentless routine, its gift shop, its machines that pulled and sucked away at hope? How could he become well, surrounded by illness and despair?

"I'll take Jay home," I said.

"Don't be silly," Dr. Block answered. "We're keeping him alive here. We help him to suffer less."

"If I take him home, maybe he'll be less sad." But I knew that I was pleading a hopelessly impractical case.

"What you don't understand is that there is a certain comfort in continuity. Jay is *used* to it here. Routine is less fatiguing and we're equipped for emergency. If you take him home, he'll be in pain. He would have to leave in a screaming ambulance. He would know."

"What do you think he knows now?" I said.

"Sometimes we know things intellectually," he said. "But not here." He patted his chest. It was such a nonmedical observation that my feelings were softened. A doctor who could refer to the human heart as a place where things are realized and experienced, rather than a vital organ simply doing its mechanical job.

"He has to know everything soon," I said.

Dr. Block made some nervous little gestures, touched and patted the clock and the pens on his desk. "Yes, I think now," he said. "Yes."

"Then we tell him." We. Somehow we had become allies in this threat to Jay's innocence. We both waited then, arranging thoughts into words, and began awkwardly to speak at the same time. I smiled at the awkwardness, and Dr. Block, looking grateful, smiled back. "Go ahead," he said.

"No, you," I insisted.

He cleared his throat and opened his hands on the desk blotter. "Would you like me to tell him?" he asked.

Ah, easy, easy. That offscreen movie scene. While I

hold my fingers in my ears and say *wah wah wah* until it's over. Eyes shut, breath held. Is it all over?

"No," I said.

"Oh." He was clearly relieved. "Then you . . . ?"

I nodded. Me. I. Myself. I could not imagine doing it, could not visualize the moment and the act. But I could not imagine anyone else doing it either. Certainly not Dr. Block, who was good enough, really a decent man, but a stranger to the unit that was Jay and me. Our twinship, kinship. My brother, my love. Pow! Bang! Right in the balls, in the heart. My God.

"But don't . . ." Dr. Block said. "We don't want to make it irrevocable . . ."

"But it is!" I said. "It is! There *is* nothing. Why can't we decide once and for all if he's to be treated like a baby or like a man?"

To my surprise there were tears in Dr. Block's eyes. "There isn't an easy way," he said. "Don't you think I know?"

"Why don't you do something then, why don't you perform miracles in this damned mystical place?" My voice was shrill and Dr. Block's secretary opened the door and looked in.

He waved her away with his hand.

"I'm sorry," I said, not feeling sorry at all, only dull and resigned.

"Do you want something for yourself?" he asked.

I shook my head and stood up.

He rushed from behind his desk so that he could open the door for me.

26

I wanted to do it while he was still able to walk. It seemed *immoral* somehow to tell a dying man the miserable and imminent truth when he was helpless, lying down in the very path of the words. Maybe I expected him to be able to run, believed that I could give him a fighting chance. Driving to the hospital I remembered old movies where the girl came to the hideout and warned the rotten but lovable crook that the law was coming. Sometimes she said, Give yourself up, sweetheart. They'll get you in the end. Other times she said, Run for it. You still have a chance.

I was supposed to tell Jay that too. There's always a chance. It seemed like the most terrible of lies. He could look in the mirror, couldn't he? He could see the truth in the wasting of himself, in the way he *felt*. How do you feel? Fine. How do *you* feel? I'm dying.

My hands and feet were cold, even though the heater blasted away. Maybe Jay would make it easier for me. He knows already, I told myself. How could he not know? It was just a matter of acknowledgment now. I know that you know that I know. That sort of crap. Oh Jesus. I had read it somewhere once. *They* always know. They. An unfortunate exclusive club of mortals. He was like his father, would be like his father, would be dust.

"That was the first blow to my innocence," he told me in one of our earliest night talks. "When my father died. It's like an old movie in my head that I can roll out whenever I want to. Sometimes when I *don't* even want to."

"You were in school, weren't you," I said, helping him to begin.

"Yes. They called me down to the principal's office. Boy, in those days it really meant something. The principal had never spoken to me before. He was as remote and glorified as the president."

"Knowing you, I'll bet you thought you had done something wrong," I said.

"The worst. What the hell could they have on me? I did my homework. I paid my G.O. money."

"You played with yourself."

"Not in *school*, kiddo. Anyway, Dr. Summers called me down to his office. They all had a doctorate then. His secretary was an old lady in orthopedic shoes. She called me James and I didn't correct her, but I felt relieved. They had the wrong kid!"

"Oh you sweet dummy," I said. "Then what happened?"

" 'Go inside, James,' " she said. "I can still see that dumb kid opening the door, a frosted glass door with gilt letters on it. Dr. Summers sat behind a big desk that was loaded with papers and books. He wore eyeglasses and he had silver-gray hair. The PTA mothers thought he was a knockout."

"Then what happened?"

"That was it. He told me. *He* called me by my right name. He kept that desk between us and he told me."

"Oh Jay."

"Yeah. I didn't believe him for just a minute. But Jesus, he was the *principal*. The flag was right there over his shoulder, and my father was dead on the job."

"He didn't suffer," I said, as if I were commenting on fresh news.

"No, but I did. My innocence did."

His innocence. Pulling into the parking lot at the hospital, I thought about that and about what I had to do now, without a doctorate or a flag or any other symbol of strength or authority.

It was old home week in the hospital room. Martin and his parents were there, a man from the television studio was visiting Jay, and in the corner of the room two strangers in coveralls wrestled with the vent of the heating unit. "Be out of here in a minute, folks," one of them said, and he knocked on metal with a hammer, as if for emphasis.

Into that chaos I smiled at Jay, who winked back. Does a dying man who *knows* wink at his wife, smile at his friends, endure hammering and visitors, the whole selfish business of the surviving world? It didn't seem possible. Jay wasn't such a good actor. It was hard for us to hide anything from each other. Without thinking about it, we always sent out signals and clues of what we were feeling. Yet there we were. The man from the studio relinquished his seat to me, still laughing about something Jay had said to him. Potted plants languished on the windowsills, Martin's father filed away at my brain with his voice.

"How do you feel?" I said idiotically to Jay, and then I kissed him, forestalling an answer.

"Not so hot," he admitted, as we separated.

The man from the studio found his coat on a low shelf and said that he was leaving. I envied him his freedom to go and at the same time I wished that he would stay. I couldn't speak to Jay in front of anyone else and now that it had to be done, now that I had decided to just *do* it, I wanted more time, delays, distractions. But I couldn't remember the man's name, even as I thought of seductive words to keep him in the room. I noticed with sharp attention a shiny place on the lapel of his suit jacket and I said, "Please don't go yet. It's early." But it sounded only courteous, the perfunctory remark of a hostess who really wants to do the dishes and go to bed.

"We'll walk you to the elevator," I said, and Jay lifted himself from the bed and put his robe and slippers on. Doing those simple things seemed to require a real and deliberate effort on his part that made me want to hurry him along, to push his arms through the sleeves, the way you do to a small child with whom you've lost patience. The other man watched too, with a certain fascination, but none of us said anything.

We walked down the hall at Jay's new slow pace and when we came to the elevator I had changed my mind again. I wanted the man to go quickly, to make his escape taking with him his small, inconsequential talk, his shiny lapels that made me feel so sad.

When he was gone and Jay turned again in the direction of his room, I put my hand on his arm. "Wait," I said. "Let's not go back there yet."

His look was questioning and I tried to explain. "I want to be alone with you."

"Oh, yeah?" Jay said, out of the corner of his mouth,

but it was a small weak joke that didn't seem to help either of us.

"Let's try the other end of the hall, the solarium," I said. All the way there I was terribly aware of the people everywhere: patients, visitors, aides, nurses. It was a goddam circus. Maybe I should put it off, I thought, and try to get permission to come up during the day when no one else was around. How could I say something like that without privacy? How could I say it anyway?

There was a cramp in my chest as if I had been running instead of trying to walk very slowly and not get there ahead of Jay. "Well, here we are," I said, when we were indeed there, in the large room at the end of the hall. It wasn't very busy that night, and there were two empty couches at the farthest corner of the room. Here? I thought. Now? Us? What if he screamed, or made a terrible scene? What if he cried, fainted, bellowed? What if I did? Oh God, what if?

We sat down, sharing one cushion of the smaller couch. The other people seemed far away and out of focus, like people in the background of a photograph. He knows, I told myself, with one last desperate surge of hope, and then I looked up and saw his eyes. They seemed strange, like the eyes of someone I had never met. There was no meaning, no message in their expression. He looked merely quizzical, expectant.

Maybe it's the drugs, I thought. Personality changes happen. Everybody knows that. Maybe the drugs had dulled his senses a little, and it wouldn't have the same horrendous meaning. Maybe I was crazy.

"Jay," I said. Our hands joined, automatically finding one another in my lap. I took a deep difficult breath, sending out signals wildly like a sailor on a doomed ship.

But Jay just sat there, not willing to cooperate at all.

"Jay," I said again. "I saw Doctor Block."

Still he waited, silent.

"He *asked* me to come in. Jay?"

His hand was passive in mine, but his eyes were beginning to change, the pupils contracting to black points. It was a retreat. Run for it, sweetheart. You still have a chance.

His head tilted slightly now as if he found it difficult to hear me.

"We talked about the tests," I said. Oh help me.

But he seemed to draw slightly away from me, from this unsolicited news.

"It's not so good, darling." Please.

He started, like someone jolted from a dream. "What in hell are you *saying*, Sandy?"

"It's not *good*," I said again.

He looked quickly around the room, his eyes darting like those of a schoolboy ready to cheat on an exam.

I followed his glance. No one was looking at us. People were leaving the solarium. We were going to be alone.

Jay looked back at me again, his face full of terrible belief. "He *told* you that? Block told you that?"

I nodded, gripping his hand against the trembling that had begun. "Jay, listen, darling. He said there's research going on this very minute. There are remissions, you know . . ."

"Oh God. Oh shit," he said. "Where is it? Is it everywhere?" He was terrified, terrifying.

I put my other hand against the pain in my chest. "Marrow," I whispered.

His eyes widened, shut for a moment and then fastened me down again. "So this is the whole thing," he said, and he dropped my hand, as if *that* was what had betrayed him.

"Please darling. Don't," I said, not even knowing what I meant. Don't what? Don't mourn for yourself? Don't rage or grieve? How did I dare tell him what to do? Give yourself up, sweetheart. They'll get you in the end.

I thought that the other questions would come then: how long do I have? Have you told anyone? What about pain? Will it be very bad? I braced myself, but he didn't say anything at all. And he didn't touch me again then, not even absently.

I felt even worse than I had before. It was as if I had killed him myself, or tried to, only inflicting a terrible wound. Bang bang, you're almost dead. My love, my dearest.

I didn't know what to do now in this reversal of roles. It was always Jay who had wrung whatever goodness there was out of me at the same time that he protected me from the worst of myself with the fierce concentration of his love. Now *I* had to protect *him*, save him at least from the monster of his fear, if I couldn't save him from death itself.

"Jay," I said. "I *love* you, darling." As if that mattered. As if anything mattered.

But it did. We turned at the same moment, colliding painfully in the desperate need to hold and to be held. We made sounds against one another, small anguished sounds that I would always remember.

When it was possible to be quiet again we stood together, and now it seemed *natural* for me to move slowly, as if I had become a part of Jay, of his cancer, his knowledge, his very being.

"Don't come back now," he whispered, at the elevator. "Go home."

"All right," I said, feeling all the unsaid words crowding around us. I *had* to do it. Forgive me. Love me. Don't give up the ship. Remember faith and fucking hope and charity. Remember.

The elevator came. Someone in a wheelchair waited inside it, looked up at us with saintly patience. So we kissed briefly, a peck really, and I took the last of his innocence and went home.

27

That night I had an erotic dream. I should have known that something disturbing was in store because I fell asleep so easily. It was as if I had been taken by force, without effort or will on my part. When I woke again it was almost five o'clock in the morning. I was still dazed with sleep, and the process of remembering began slowly. I felt strangely happy and expectant. The dream. I remembered it first with my body, an urgent memory between my legs and across my breasts. Then I remembered everything else all at once. Jay. My God, it was true. But the erotic feeling was still there, a restless demanding heat that transcended grief and love.

There had been a man in the dream, nameless and faceless. No, not really faceless, just no one I consciously knew or could identify. But people wear clever disguises in dreams and can be anybody. I had provoked him, urged him on, feeling terribly excited, but then I woke before I was satisfied, even before he entered me. Maybe it was Jay, I thought, wanting to be loyal, but I knew that it wasn't. There had been an illicit quality, a stealthiness to my urging. Now. Oh, do it. Dreams. If I were going to somebody for help, for therapy, I would bring the dream with me and try to understand it. But what was there to understand? Everyone needs sex. The feeling of deprivation is instinctual, isn't it?

Why didn't I see it through, damn it. It was only a dream. God, I felt so lonely then. Love. Did Jay still have erections now? What did he do with them? I had a picture in my head of all those little cubicles, the high metal beds ringed off by white curtains, and the patients inside working themselves off in tenuous privacy. Did they pull out tubes and needles in their frenzy? Did the nurses and aides leave them in peace? Or did they bring them aid? First aid. Help.

I lay on my belly and I wedged Jay's pillow there between my thighs. Love. I let the stranger into the room and he was clever, light-footed and graceful. Come, I urged him again, trying to remember the language of the dream. Why didn't I imagine Jay now instead? Never mind, I thought, it's only a game, an escape. It doesn't matter. I let Mr. X. keep his face in shadow, and I commanded him to kiss me everywhere. It was all right, this work of fantasy. No one gets hurt, right? Between one consenting adult, ha ha. It's done all the time, in prisons, even with the night-lights blazing, or in hospitals, making bed charts tremble, done to the rhythm of rubber-soled shoes prowling the floors.

Mr. X. was interested, but lazily reluctant. It was up to me and I was full of invention and direction. Here, do this, that. I guided his hands, his mouth, whispered encouragement. He had no imagination, wasn't like Jay, wasn't Jay, wasn't. He did my bidding, though, until I breathed a great final gasp of relief and wished him away.

28

"Joseph," I said. "Just tell me one thing. What do you hear on that radio that's so much better than the real world?"

Joseph looked surprised. "This?" he asked, holding up the small black rectangle, from which anguished cries of sound emerged.

I nodded. "What do you *hear*?"

He smiled engagingly. "Oh—music, the games, talk shows." He held the radio out to me. "Here. Do you want to listen?"

I held up my arm as if he had threatened to strike me. "No. No thanks. I was just curious. You seem so involved."

"Yeah," he said. "Well, just like this one station, people call up all day and give their opinions. Then other people call up and disagree with them. It's *educational*."

"Oh," I said.

"Like today," he continued. "They're all talking about

clothing, whether it's natural for women and men to dress the same. Other times they talk about bigger stuff: integration and unions and war. You really learn a lot. Sometimes real crackpots call up and start yelling and screaming." Joseph laughed. "Yesterday this woman called up that wanted animals to wear, you know, underwear. A real old lady. She said it would set a good example for young people and keep the streets clean at the same time."

"That's an idea," I said, and Joseph looked at me quizzically, not sure how to take it.

"I'm only fooling," I said. "I love naked dogs."

"Oh," he said, relieved. "Then I hear the top tunes and people call up and give their opinions about records they hear." He put the radio against the side of his head again, closing the conversation.

On the way to the hospital, I listened to the station that Joseph had told me about.

"Hello, this is Jeff Lewis. Good afternoon." Brisk, intimidating.

A pause. Sound of breathing. Then, "Jeff, is that you, Jeff?"

"Good afternoon, this is Jeff Lewis speaking. Go ahead, please."

"Jeff?" the voice said. "You sound different on the telephone. You sound, I don't know, younger."

"Will you please shut your radio off while you are speaking to me, Madam."

"Oh, Jeff, I'm sorry. I forgot. Just a minute." Pause. "Okay, Jeff. I'm back."

"Go ahead please, Madam. There are other calls waiting."

"Oh. Well. I almost forgot what I wanted to say. You were talking before to that man from Staten Island? He said that pretty soon nobody will be able to tell men from women and then the human race will die out?"

"Yes?" said Jeff Lewis.

"Well, I'm a person of years. I won't say how many. What that man from Staten Island doesn't understand is that the young people own the world."

"Madam, I don't get your point."

"I mean if young people want to dress funny, men with pocketbooks and girls with suits, we have to go along with the tide. A hundred years from now a man with a pocketbook will be *old-fashioned.*"

"Yes, well, thank you for calling. The lines are open, folks. That number is 222-1144. One more time. 222-1144. Hello, Jeff Lewis speaking."

"Hi Jeff, I'd like to talk to you about shock treatment for patients in state hospitals."

"That was a show we did last week, sir. Today we're talking about unisex, the practice of men and women dressing alike."

"But what's more important? It seems to me that we should concentrate on the more important issues in life."

"Thank you for your opinion, sir. But we follow a certain structure here and today we are talking about unisex."

"Talk, talk yourself sick, you idiot," the man said. "Drop dead! I—"

"I have another call here. Hello, this is Jeff Lewis. Go ahead please."

"Jeff, that woman that called up before that man from Staten Island has the wrong idea. The young own the world *only* and I stress that word *only* if we give it to them. What's wrong with the old ways, what's wrong with the kind of life our parents and our grandparents gave us? I remember a decent world, Jeff, with decent hardworking people in it. Black, white, pink, green. We didn't always have it so easy, Jeff. But there was a sense of decency. That's the key word, here. Decency. I remember a family sitting down to dinner with respect and love for each other. My father held the door open for my mother, we never took one bite until she sat down at that table. Look at the Chinese race, Jeff, if you want to see respect for old people, if you want . . ."

"Thank you very much for your opinion, Madam. This is the place to sound off, folks. This is your host, Jeff Lewis, and the number to call is . . ."

Then I was driving into the parking lot, past the places reserved for doctors only, past the massive air-conditioning unit, past the kitchen, where I could see women in white caps lifting huge pots. I parked and went upstairs to Jay's room. Martin's mother and father were just taking Martin, in a wheelchair, for a ride down the corridor.

It was the first time that Jay and I had been alone since I'd told him. "Sandy," he said. "We have to talk. Come on, sweetie, we have to talk sometime."

I sat on his bed, my legs dangling. He took my hands between his and pressed them lightly. "I'm tired. Don't make me do all the work."

"Jay," I said.

"But we have to make plans for the kids, for your future."

"You sound like an insurance salesman," I said.

But Jay didn't smile. "You know where the policies are. There'll be something extra from the union and whatever is in the pension now. God, we were never savers, Sandy."

I thought of the things we spent money on, of clothes hanging round-shouldered on hangers at home, of meals, eaten, digested, eliminated. Toys, magazines, cameras, radios, electric blankets. What would I do with Jay's clothing?

"Speak to Murray. He'll want you to invest carefully in some things. Blue chips, mutual funds. The market's so crazy." He drew a terribly deep breath and put a hand to his chest.

"Shhh," I said.

"Sandy, I'm sorry."

"Oh, shhh. Don't." I leaned over and put my head against his chest, lightly, holding back my weight. I could hear the hollow thrumming of his heartbeat and an echo of my own crazy pulse.

"I don't believe it. Not really. I say it but I don't believe it, as if I'm talking about somebody else." His voice reverberated painfully against my ear.

"Me too," I whispered.

"The thing is I always thought that I would get old. I *worried* about it. How we would look, how hard it would be."

"Oh Jay," I said. "I only want to be with you."

"And the kids . . ." His voice broke.

I sat up and looked into his eyes. "Jay, what about Mona?"

"You never said anything to her? You never wrote?"

I shook my head.

He breathed another long shuddering sigh. "Don't tell her," he said.

I thought he meant never, to never tell her. "I *can't* . . ." I began.

"No, listen. Call her when it's too late."

"Jay, she has a right . . ."

"Sandy, if you call her now, she'll come right here. You know Mona. Sandy, I couldn't look at her. When my father died . . . Her face is like a broken heart. I couldn't

164

stand it," and then he began to cry, in harsh broken sounds that I had never heard before.

"I won't. I promise, I won't. Jay, sweetheart, I promise."

He grew quiet again and his hand slipped around my waist.

Then Martin and his parents came back into the room. They found me with my face against Jay's throat, with his hand under my sweater, cooling the skin of my back.

"Uh-oh," Martin's father said. "Maybe we should have knocked."

But his mother took it all in, the red eyes, the sorrow that hung in the room like something visible.

Poor Martin looked frightened. Had he ever seen his parents embrace, even in joy? "Love in bloom," I said.

"They vant to be alone," Martin's father croaked. He helped Martin to climb back into bed.

Then we all talked, idle, drifting chatter, half listening to one another and to the other sounds around us, until the shadows grew long in the room, and it was time to go home again.

29

The postcard was printed:

Dear Mrs. (and here my name had been typed in).
*It is now six months since your last gynecological
checkup. An appointment has been arranged for you
on Thursday, January 23rd, at 10* A.M. *If for some
reason you cannot keep this appointment, please
notify this office at least 48 hours before the scheduled
time.*

The same postcards always came twice a year to my
mother and me. We arrange to have our appointments
on the same day and in the past we had gone shopping
together and out for lunch. I called my mother and told
her that I didn't think I was up to it now, that I would
go at some other time. (Thinking—never again, what difference does it make, who cares.) We hung up and a few
minutes later she called back and gave me a long lecture
about taking care of myself for the sake of the children,

that I owed it to Jay to be both mother and father to them, that my body was a sacred temple, that she hated to go by herself—sometimes she felt a little dizzy afterwards, you read in the paper about not waiting too long, because God knows what's going on inside you, God forbid, and I couldn't stop living, even if I felt like it.

Finally I said, "All right, all right," and she breathed a long whistling sigh. "Tootsie," she said. "I know how you feel."

We traveled together as we always did. I drove to the beauty shop and honked the horn two times.

My father came out with a hairbrush in his hand. Inscribed on his smock in an intricate scrolled script was *Mr. B*. He reached in the window to touch my cheek and I saw that his hand trembled slightly. "She'll be out in a minute," he said. "She's just getting her coat."

"Go inside, Daddy. It's cold."

"I'm all right," he insisted. "I can take the cold." But he backed away anyway, waving, and went into the store. Then in a few minutes they appeared together at the doorway and my father reached into his pocket for his wallet. He gestured briefly toward the car and then he gave her some money.

My mother ran in those funny choppy steps, as if her legs were tied together, and then she sat down beside me in the car. "We shouldn't have had a Thursday," she said. "It's a busy day for us. They should have given us a Monday or a Tuesday."

"Ma," I said. "I was willing to change."

"Tootsie, some things can't be put off." She lowered the visor mirror to look at herself, leaning close and squinting. She lifted her lips in a terrible leer and shook her head. "Don't neglect your teeth," she said.

At the clinic we went into adjoining curtained booths and undressed. We put on the paper gowns and slippers provided for us and then we opened the curtains and sat on the little stools and waited.

A nurse came by and said that they were a little delayed and that we would have to wait about fifteen minutes. "So just relax," she advised.

"Ha!" my mother said. Then she reached behind her and brought her pocketbook onto her lap. "I want to give you something."

"Ma," I said. "We have medical insurance. The network has been very generous."

"Take it for Daddy. He specifically said."

The paper gowns rustled as I held out my hand. "Tell him thank you. Thank you both."

"I always hate this," she said, looking around.

"Waiting?"

"The whole business. I know they don't even think about us, the doctors. Not as women. But it makes me nervous, anyway, to put my feet up like that." She shuddered.

"It only takes a few minutes." In my head I lie on the bed at home, my arms opened. Oh come into me. Your voice enters me. Come in. Jay parts my legs like brambles in a forest and goes through.

"Yeah, well . . ." my mother said.

"Think about something else. Pretend you're in Paris and Doctor Miller is your lover."

"Some lover."

"Pretend you're at the dentist's. Open wide now, dear."

"You!" She blushed. "Listen, do you know what I do? I shut my mind off completely."

"I wish that I could do that."

"I thought you didn't mind the examination."

"Not that," I said. "I just wish that I didn't have to think."

"My poor girl," she said, and she patted my hand. She looked down at her bare legs, embroidered with blue veins. "Older people should go first."

"No," I said. "Nobody should go, ever."

"Don't be crazy. It would be like the BMT in the rush hour. As you get older, you change, anyway." She stood up and stepped back into her booth. She crooked her finger. "Come here for a second."

I walked into her booth and she reached up and pulled the curtain. Then she parted the gown and lifted it. "I once had a beautiful figure," she said. "Look at that."

Her skin was mottled pink and white, as if she had just come from a hot bath. Her breasts were two pale tilting moons. There were sharp red marks where her girdle had held her and the thin line of an old scar ran across her belly, disappearing into the sparse, graying bush. She pointed to the trembling flesh of her thigh.

"Ma," I said, "you still . . ."

"Feel that. Just feel that."

I reached out and touched her skin briefly.

She smiled triumphantly. *"That's* what happens!" She lowered the gown and opened the curtain again.

I went back to my own booth and sat down.

"It happens to everyone," she said. "Things don't work so well anymore."

"Don't you feel well? Is it Daddy?"

She shrugged. *"Everybody* slows down. You can't do all the things you could *always* do."

Suddenly I realized what she was talking about. I leaned over to look at her and she was staring down into the open pocketbook in her lap. I wanted to say something compassionate, as if she had just told me of the sudden death of a friend, but I found that I couldn't speak.

"Some people think that they are going to live forever,

that time is never going to get in their way." Her mouth closed in a narrow furrow.

I wanted to say, "Forgive him then." I felt terribly disloyal, knowing this news of my father. I thought of him looking at his own reflection above the head of a seated customer, combing his moustache, sucking in his belly and then letting it out again with a long hissing sigh. I imagined that she thought he had met a just punishment. I wanted to say, "Forgive him," but my mother snapped her pocketbook shut with a final click that ended the conversation.

Then the nurse came down the hall, humming a tune. "Okay girls," she said. "You're on."

30

I was never really afraid of the basement in our building. There are women who make their husbands or teen-age sons go with them when they use the laundry, or they travel in groups, like flocks of frightened birds. For me, nothing, no danger lurked in the shadows of those stippled gray walls.

We had less laundry now. It seemed a pitiable pile without Jay's clothing among ours. I sat in the straight-backed peeling kitchen chair facing the dryers, with an open book in my lap. In front of me the clothes tossed and whirled as if swept by a fitful wind. Every few minutes I raised my eyes from the book, unable to concentrate, and saw bits of yellow, blue, or white: Paul's baseball pajamas, my own nightgown. I could hear motors starting and then stopping, water screaming in the pipes overhead, and the whine of the elevator ascending. Somewhere in the distance doors slammed, and muted voices spoke.

Then the elevator descended again and there were footsteps in the corridor leading to the storage room. I stood up and looked through the doorway.

Estrella Caspar was there, her arms filled with bulging shopping bags. She seemed to be costumed for a starring role in a futuristic movie. Whatever she was wearing was made of a dazzling vinyl, reflecting the lights in the room. She wore large dark glasses, goggles actually. Her hair rose in a wild black cloud and an Indian headband was pulled across her forehead. "Oh, it's *you*," she said, and she rushed ahead toward the storage lockers.

I went back to my vigil at the dryers. There were ten minutes left on the timer. I could hear the metallic echoes of a locker being slammed shut, and then her footsteps again as she returned.

This time she paused in the doorway. "It's snowing again," she said. "I'm going to wear my brown patent leather boots . . ."

"Is it sticking?" I asked.

But she was bending over now, peering into the window of the spinning dryer. She turned her head in a circular motion, in playful imitation of the tossing clothes. "Hey, this is even better than the late show!" she said, and her birdcall laugh reverberated everywhere. Then she stooped to look at me, lifting the dark glasses to her forehead. Her eyes were like something seen through a microscope, so terrible were they in detail. Her false lashes were thick and black like the enlarged legs of insects. "You could do something," she said. "You should change your lipstick."

Automatically, my hand came up to my mouth. If I had been wearing any lipstick, I had already eaten it off.

"Blond hair and fair skin, you should use something in the coral family." She pulled a huge leather fringed pouch from her shoulder, opened it, and leaned her head inside. "Here, wait a minute, I'll show you." She pulled things out impatiently, scattering them on top of the dryers. Out came a thick pink wallet, a pair of blue satin slippers with furry pompons on the toes, keys, scented crumpled tissues, a round, framed mirror, and makeup: tubes, compacts, boxes rolling this way and that, powder spilling in a fine pale snow. "It's in here. God, I'll be late. They'll kill me."

"Then don't," I said. "It's all right."

"No no no, it's right here. It's perfect. Ah," she said finally and she withdrew a tube of lipstick, pulled off its cover with a flourish, and rolled it open. "Here," forcing it under my eyes. "Coral Dreams," she said, and I could feel her breath and smell it, a stale lavender scent. Or was it the lipstick? Only a stub of a lipstick, actually. "You can have it," she said. "Here, here," pushing it into my hand.

The book had fallen to the floor. "Thank you," I whispered.

"It can change your outlook," she said. She winked, and pushed the goggles down, hiding her eyes. "Use Lemon Ice underneath for a base. You could be good-looking yourself."

"Thank you," I said again.

She began to spill the makeup and slippers and keys back into the pouch. I picked things up that had rolled onto the floor and handed them to her. She hummed, with her lips pursed, and examined herself in the mirror.

The dryer turned more slowly now and then came to a stop, the last garment floating weightlessly to the bottom of the basket. "Done!" I said brightly, but she had turned her back and I could hear her shoes clicking on the tiled floor as she made her way back to the elevator.

I looked down at the lipstick in the palm of my hand. I thought I might write something on the wall near the dryer with it. Something in keeping with what was already scribbled there: names, dates, curses, threats. What? Fuck the world? Jay and Sandy forever? In this catacomb, poor

Christians died . . . I dropped the lipstick into the lint-filled darkness behind the dryer and then I began to empty it of my laundry.

I went upstairs and found Harry sobbing into the sofa cushion and Paul sucking his thumb on the opposite end of the sofa. Joseph was on his hands and knees with his head under the skirt of the upholstered chair. His voice came out muffled and strained. "I'm looking for it, Harry. We'll *find* it, Harry." But this only seemed to be a cue for Harry to howl with more passion.

"What's the matter?" I asked, and Joseph backed up from under the chair, banging his head. "Oh, I didn't even hear you come in. It's that stupid turtle."

I sat down and Harry rushed me, pushing his wet face into my lap. "My t-turtle," he sobbed, gasping and spilling a new flood of tears and saliva.

"What happened?"

"It's g-gone."

"It can't be gone. Turtles can't open doors."

"That's what I told him," Joseph said. "Turtles can't open doors."

"Where's the bowl?"

Joseph brought me the bowl with the plastic palm tree on its center island. Only one turtle, and that one withdrawing from the environment, was there.

"Which one is missing?" I asked. Harry had never even named them, although Paul made up new and endearing terms for them all the time. Honey, Lulu, Bingo, Poppy, Moony.

"The one with the soft shell," Joseph said.

"The best one," Harry wailed.

"We'll find it, baby," I told him. "Turtles walk so slowly." I moved my arms, turtle fashion, swimming through a dense atmosphere.

174

Joseph cupped the side of his mouth. "I looked every-where," he whispered.

"Now, stop it, Harry," I insisted. "We have to think. Did you take it downstairs with you when you went to the park?"

He shook his head.

"Did you take it out of the bowl today at all? Did you, Paul?"

Paul withdrew his thumb with a popping sound, looked at its wet puckered flesh, and shook his head.

"Okay, so it climbed out of the bowl and it jumped off the table. It's somewhere in the house and we'll find it."

Joseph whispered in another aside. "If it doesn't starve to death, if it doesn't get stepped on first."

Harry resumed his weeping.

"We'll put food out for it," I said, inspired. "Like they did for the elves in the story. Go get the turtle food."

"I don't want to step on it," Harry said, without moving.

"Take off your shoes. Then you can't hurt it. You won't step on it anyway. It's hiding someplace."

"When we lived in the Bronx, in the old place," Joseph said, "I had a hamster? Well, it got loose from the cage and we couldn't find it. Boy, we searched for that hamster for two weeks. Well, P.S. we found it all right. It climbed into this hole in the hall closet and it starved to death. Did that stink! Even the people next door could smell it in their closet. They went yelling to the super. It was all stiff, with its eyes open . . ."

"Ixnay, ixnay," I said.

"Huh? Oh yeah. Well, a hamster isn't like a turtle. Hamsters are known for getting into walls like that."

Harry came back with the little box of turtle food. He began to shake it out in the corner of the room.

"No, wait a minute," I said. "We have to put the food

in water. Remember what it says on the box?" I went into the kitchen and gathered four jar lids and filled them with water. We sprinkled a fine shower of turtle food into each of them, and then set them out in the dark places under furniture.

"Well, that's that," I said.

"He'll be back tomorrow, you'll see, Harry," Joseph said, as he was leaving.

Then I bathed the children together, letting them play roughly and splash, secretly watching their bodies, the small dangling bells of their sex.

Later, when I lay sleepless in the very center of the bed, Paul cried out.

I went into their room and bent over him. "What's the matter, honey?"

"I'm afraid of the turtle," he said.

"What? Afraid of that little turtle? He can't hurt you."

"I don't want him to come into my bed."

"Paulie," I said. "Turtles can't climb up on a big high bed. They don't even know how to climb."

He was still whimpering and I said, "Do you want me to come into bed with you for a while?" I lay down beside him and he locked himself against my side as if he had been pulled there by suction. A small fire at which to warm myself. In the middle of the night, I awoke from a dream, instantly forgotten, and tiptoed back to my own bed, looking for the turtle in my path.

We didn't find it the next day or the next, and Harry continued to grieve for it.

"Harry," I said. "You didn't even really like that turtle."

"I did."

"Sometimes you wouldn't look at it for days. Sometimes the bowl was dry. You forgot to give them food and water."

176

"I did," he said, growing sullen. "I loved it."

"Okay," I said. "I'll buy you another turtle."

"I want that one," he said. "I don't want another one."

"Harry." I touched his face, making him look at me. "Do you think about Daddy?"

"*I want that turtle!*" he said, almost without moving his lips.

"Listen, sweetheart. Daddy wants to be here. But he can't help it. He's so sick. It's not his fault. He still loves us. Do you remember he sent you that nice kangaroo from the hospital?" My God.

"*I want my turtle!*" he shrieked, shutting his eyes and forcing blood into his head until his face was a violent red.

I wanted to shake him then, to rattle his teeth and bones the way I had when he wouldn't eat. Enough anger and despair grew in me to smash furniture, to fell trees. But then he looked directly at me and I saw his rage and his sorrow and he saw mine. My arms fluttered open like wings. He moved into them and I embraced him, holding on for dear life.

31

Martin was being transferred from Jay's room to another part of the hospital. I believed that his mother had made the request. She would not meet my eyes as she busied herself at his nightstand. "Do you want these?" she asked, holding up letters and cards. "Are you going to save everything?"

Martin sat in a blue robe at the side of the bed, which had already been stripped of its bedding. He nodded in answer to his mother's questions. His father waited in the hallway, sticking his head in from time to time to say things like "How goes it?" and "How are you doing?" in his grating whisper. Martin said nothing.

His mother held up an African violet plant that had been sent by a class in Martin's school. "Why don't you take this?" she asked her husband, as his face appeared in the doorway again.

"Well excuse me," he said, going past Jay's bed. He winked, smiled, took the plant from his wife and backed out of the room. In a few minutes, he looked in again. "How goes it?" he asked.

A nurse came with a wheelchair for Martin. "Well," his mother said. "*That* looks like *that. You'll* get a little peace and quiet," she said to Jay. She walked to his bed, extending her hand. "Very nice to meet you."

"Thank you," Jay said.

The father came into the room again and, transferring the plant to his other hand, he held the empty one out to Jay and then to me. "Nice to meet you folks," he said. His hand was moist. He wiped it on the side of his jacket. "Good luck, now," he added.

Martin was wheeled to Jay's bedside. "Jay," he said, tremulous.

Jay smiled at him. "Sandy will bring the proofs of last week's takes. I'll get them to you. Remember what I said about the skylight filter."

"I will, Jay." Martin's eyes were brilliant with tears. I thought that it had done his mother no good to protect him, after all. Simply by loving, he knew the fragile thread of human relationships.

"Fair-weather friends," I said to Jay. From the hallway we could hear voices, diminishing footsteps. I shut the door and came back and sat next to him on the bed. He put his hand on my cheek and his touch was cool and light. "Sweetie," he said. "Would you do something for me?"

"You know," I said.

"Will you go in there with me for a little while?" He gestured toward the small bathroom. "I haven't seen you in such a long time. I haven't touched you." He stroked my hair. "Will you?"

The passage from the bed to the bathroom was done in the slow process of dreamwalking. Would we get there?

I locked the door behind us and while Jay leaned against the tiled wall, I pulled off my sweater and let my skirt fall in a gray puddle at my feet. He reached his hands behind me to unhook my brassiere and I wondered whose trembling had aroused the other's. "Oh," he said, as if in first discovery and I echoed, "Oh," as my breasts pressed into his hands.

"Lovely, lovely, lovely," Jay said.

I reached forward to help him with his pajamas, shutting my eyes for a moment against revelation of what had happened to him. I knew that when I opened them again I would see what was to be my real and lasting memory of Jay. No matter what happened to him from that moment. No matter how I remembered him from what seemed to be only a brief summer of moments: Jay, running with the swift power of a sketch that denotes movement and grace, Jay, wearing an erection like a banner, Jay, seen from a window, from our bed, from my place across the table.

But I looked at him, at his poor wasted flesh, with a fierce attention, committing him to remembrance in waxen colors, in that warning of the skeletal frame, in the odors that arose like sweet poisons to my nostrils.

My poor Jay, his mouth groping and his hands too light, too fragile to leave burning indelible marks. And the trembling more like a shudder that began in the earth beneath us.

I kneeled and made a carpet of our clothing on the floor, and I led him down beside me. Whose breath was that, like a rush of wind? No erection now, only a soft nervous mass that seemed to withdraw from my hand. "It will be good," I promised, and I rubbed him gently between my hands, thinking, it will be good, it will be good, letting motion fall into the rhythm of those words.

I willed it with savage concentration, with ideas of flowering things—open, newborn—soaring, and then I moved down, finding him with my mouth, my eyes still shut to enclose the fantasy.

Jay's voice came from a great distance at the first quivers and I thought that it was possible to give life this way, to recreate with my life-giving mouth, to invade him with love the way that disease had invaded him. Behind my eyes comets flashed by and I *believed* in my mouth, in my magic tongue, in my power to restore and rekindle. God—it was so easy! Now he stirred and cried my name in feral triumph and let his final warmth rush out.

32

Dear children

It is raining in Paradise. When it rains we sleep a lot. Sam is snoozing now in the other room and my head is falling over. I look out the window and I can see the ocean from here with all that water and the rain coming down heavy like drumbeats. Sometimes nature seems crazy to me. It should be raining on a desert instead.

Ho hum I am dropping off so this will be only a little shortie. Tell my boys that Grandma is thinking of them and sends them many kisses.

Nuiloha
Mona

P.S. Sam says do you want natives pulling in the fishnets or a beach scene at sunrise?

33

They came in at first with the awe and curiosity of tourists entering a church in a foreign country. They looked around them at the narrow white beds, at the dangling ropes of tubing, at the cabinets and sinks, as if they were politely acknowledging yet *another* painting of the Holy Mother and Child, yet another frayed tapestry of angels, lambs, and unicorns, eyes raised even higher than heaven.

I stood near the door as they entered and I greeted them. The women pecked at my cheeks and the men combined clumsy hugs with handshakes. I collected their words like tickets of admission. "Sandy, how are you doing? I hope we're not too late. Don't forget to call us if there's *anything* we can do."

What more could they be expected to do? They were here to offer their very blood and yet they wouldn't save Jay.

My mother and father were early and they stood uneasily behind me at the door. But their presence gave everyone a second gesture. My mother was kissed, my father's hand was pummeled and vibrated.

The men came from the television studio, and their wives were with them, some in fur coats, smelling of winter air. Neighbors from our apartment building arrived, looking shy and out of place, as if they were distaff relatives. Isabel was there with Eddie. He sniffed expectantly, like a dog, and he was pale. Mr. Caspar was there, letting himself be part of the crowd, smiling seriously.

Three attendants in appropriate white went in and out of the room, bearing beakers, trays and test tubes. Eddie watched them and I was reminded of Harry at the doctor's office, looking suspiciously at everything. What's that? What are you going to do?

An old friend from high school came in and there were cries of recognition. The awe and the curiosity were wearing off. People recognized one another and were introduced to others. Two of the announcers from the studio arrived and even the attendants stopped their bustling and whispered and pointed. It was *really* the man who brought the six o'clock news, it was *really* the one who spoke so seriously and frankly about indigestion and constipation. Their voices rose a bit and became the swarming hum heard at cocktail parties, punctuated by audible phrases. "For heaven's sake, I didn't know that you knew . . ." "This is my wife, Helen. Helen, Helen, listen this is . . ." "Well, I've been a fan of yours for . . ." "Do you remember those old screens, maybe seven inches with a magnifying glass . . ." Someone laughed in a clear high tone like the sound of glasses clinking together. "Shhhh," from someone else, remembering.

Why, I was a hostess at a cocktail party. One only had

to imagine hors d'oeuvres passed around the room and the sweet easing of whiskey, and music defying the voices. I wished I had a drink then, could move among them with a facility only remembered. How are you? What a lovely skirt. You can carry it with your height. I'm so glad you could come. Was there much traffic on the expressway? I know, that damned construction. Did you read his review in the *Times*? You look marvelous with your hair that way.

Instead, numb and dumb, in the doorway, pinching my own fingers for feeling, out of style, out of date. What was I wearing? I looked down, saw the gray skirt; the color of winter skies, of park pigeons, of dark thoughts.

Then one of the white-suited attendants began to move among them looking for volunteers. Voices grew softer. Nervous giggles. Two men from the studio went forward. On spring days Jay had played ball with them in Central Park, running on the soft damp grass, flushed, breathless. The ball arced in the air, first golden in sunlight, then dappled by the shadows of the trees. They removed their jackets and put them on hooks against the far wall. The rest of us watched as they lay down on the beds. Their wives came forward too, hung their coats alongside the men's. They removed their shoes and primped their hair with little nervous gestures. One of the women turned and smiled at me. I smiled back in encouragement, trying to remember her name. The women lay down, tugging modestly at the hems of their skirts. Their fingers were pricked for samples. The technicians moved among the beds, adjusting bottles and tubes. Behind me, someone (Eddie? My father?) gasped as the first blood ran down. Irreverently, I remembered horror movies, thunder and lightning crashing and crackling at the windows. The heroine strapped to the table.

The mad scientist racing hunched around the laboratory, his wild laughter and spittle mixing with the steaming vapor of the test tubes he carries. Ha ha, the scientist throws back his head as the heroine writhes on the table. Hee hee, I vant to sock your blodt. Oh God.

The men are sitting up now on the beds. One flashes a V-sign. My mother and father lie down when the beds are empty. A customer from the beauty shop, with a towering beehive hairdo, joins them. My father's face is moist and pale. He touches himself—his hair where it's thinning at the top, his moustache, the waistband of his trousers, his throat. All there, everything intact. If we were alone, I would hold his hand. He knows about death, on that table. My mother keeps her expression, the same always, doesn't wince or look back. I should have been like her. A great fuss is made over the beehive hairdo. The customer gestures toward my father and the technician looks appreciative, touches her own hair. My father, white and sad, winks at her, offers her a discount rate, pulls a business card from his pocket.

My father's blood comes, and my mother's. My father shuts his eyes, sending himself someplace more reasonable.

Then it is Eddie's turn and Izzy lies down beside him, touching his arm briefly so that he is able to smile, half his lip curling up. Looking at the ceiling, thinking, it's the smell I can't stand.

The others linger in an anteroom where coffee is served, heavy on the sugar. One of the women has to lie down again. Her shoes are on the floor. "I feel silly," she says. "It's probably mind over matter. But no, I've always had low blood pressure. It's true."

My father comes into the anteroom. I kiss his cool flesh. Daddy. My mother. Izzy. The neighbor from downstairs who bangs on the ceiling with a broom when the boys run.

See, I'm a good person in my heart. Takes three cubes of sugar, puts two in her purse, another in her coat pocket. Two cousins from Long Island, an uncle from Brooklyn, rolling down his sleeve. Eddie comes in and waits for his reward. Thank you, Eddie. You're a good friend. Good dog, good boy. Thanks, everybody. Blow kisses. I don't know what to say. I vant to sock your blodt. Tenk you everybodty.

The coats on again. "Can I drop you off?" "It was terrific to see you again, I mean . . ." "Ohhh, it's snowing again." Kiss kiss. "Call me, will you call me if you need anything? Do you promise?" "Thank you, thanks for coming." My hostess gown flutters at my ankles. It was a success. "I can't tell you . . . Good-bye I only wish . . . I know . . . Good-bye good-bye."

And then I lie down too, and the needle enters. Help help. Ha ha my proud beauty. Don't struggle. I'm only going to inject you with this secret formula . . .

34

That next week Jay's condition began to deteriorate so rapidly that it seemed that acknowledgment had been a form of surrender. We had said yes, and there were hemorrhages from the nose and from the rectum, insidious but steady bleeding from the gums, and long periods of sleep from which he emerged bruised in the flesh and in the spirit. Sometimes dogs stalked in Jay's dreams, with teeth bared and haunches rolling under their skin. Nothing was fastened down anymore. Buildings careened and lurched and the sky splintered and fell. Uninvited guests arrived and left inside his head and he shouted without making a sound, and forced himself to surface again.

There were only a few visitors now to his new room, a small monk's cell in which he would carry out his retreat. We whispered there as if we entered a darkened auditorium or a place of worship. Once Jay woke briefly from dozing and said, "I can't hear you," although no one had spoken.

My mother came there, tiptoeing and trying to look at ease with her heart. Izzy sat at the bedside to relieve me and she seemed thinner in the shadows of that room, as if she were reduced by what she saw there. Yet people still called and said, "How is he?" I could not imagine what they wanted to know. Not the clinical details of dying, not news of additional equipment brought daily, until Jay seemed readied for some marvelous scientific feat, for propulsion into the outer realms of the universe.

My father drove there with me one Friday. It was raining and we ran from the parking lot to the entrance under the large black bloom of his umbrella. "Daddy," I said. "Every day he looks worse. Try not to be surprised when you see him." I wondered who it was I protected.

Jay was awake when we came into the room, with huge fetal eyes watching the doorway. He smiled and raised his hand slightly in greeting. "Mr. B.," he said, and my father's Adam's apple made a rapid passage up and down his throat. We nudged one another gently toward the one bedside chair, and finally I sat down, and my father positioned himself against the wall facing the bed, assuming a casual pose with his arms folded and one foot crossed in front of the other.

"Do you need anything?" I whispered to Jay, wincing against the possibility of some final rage—yes, new blood, another chance, a fucking life.

His hand came up and rasped against his jaw. "I feel like a slob," he said in his new voice. "That fellow who used to shave me doesn't come anymore."

"I'll speak to him. I'll look for him right now." I motioned my father into the chair and went out into the hall to look for the barber. A nurse sat at the station, writing in a ledger. She reminded me of illustrations of nurses I remembered in children's books on careers for girls. She didn't look up for a long time and then she said, "Yes?" briefly, without real interest.

"I'm looking," I began, and realized that I still whispered. In a louder voice I said, "I'm looking for the barber. My husband wants to be shaved."

"Who is your husband?" she asked.

I thought she knew who I was, had seen me a hundred times. "Mr. Kaufman. In 516. He said the barber hasn't been in there."

She looked into the ledger, turning the pages. "You know, we try to disturb our terminal patients as little as possible."

"But it won't disturb him. He wants to be shaved. He feels uncomfortable this way."

"The barber is not assigned to your husband's ward. He's gone for the day anyway."

"Will he give him a shave tomorrow?"

"Tomorrow?"

I tapped my fingers on the desk.

"The barber's not assigned to your husband's ward. I just told you that."

"But then you said that he was gone for the day anyway. I thought that you meant that he would come at another time."

"I'm afraid that I didn't mean that at all. I meant what I said in the first place." Then she put her pen down and folded her hands. "Ah, why don't you just let him be?" she said.

I felt a grievous rage against her and a terrible weariness right on its heels. I walked back down the hall and tried to catch my father's eye without coming into the room. He saw me and murmured something to Jay. Then he came outside. "What's the matter?"

190

"The barber won't come here. That bitch down the hall won't let him."

He peered down the corridor and saw the peak of her cap haloed in the light as she leaned over her desk. "Do you want me to talk to her?"

Oh God, did he think he could *seduce* her into getting the barber for Jay? "No, Daddy. I'll tell Jay something. I'll tell him the barber is sick too. I'll tell him that beards are all the rage."

"Now take it easy," he said. "Listen, *I'll* do it."

"What?" I had lost track of what we had been saying.

"I'll shave Jay."

"You can't."

"Why not? I mean I'm a barber and Jay wants it. Tell him the regular barber is off duty and that I request the honor."

Tears came to my eyes. I squeezed his hand.

"Give me the keys," he said. "I'll get the stuff from the shop and I'll be back in a little while."

I went into Jay's room. "Guess what?" I said. "Daddy is going to shave you."

Jay looked interested. "Mr. B.?"

I nodded. "The barber is gone for the day. Daddy just went out to get his equipment." We could hear footsteps and voices from the corridor and I put my finger to my lips. It was as if we shared a wonderful conspiracy to spring him from prison.

My father came back later carrying a shopping bag. He put it on the chair and rubbed his hands together. "Shut the door," he said.

I looked both ways first. "All clear."

He had everything with him: a snowy apron for Jay, his own weathered shaving brush, a mug of soap, and a straight-edged razor that he held up for us to see with an almost maniacal pleasure. "That's a beauty," he said. "I'd like to see what this guy at the hospital uses."

I wanted to say, Get on with it, for God's sake. Someone will come. It's only a shave.

But it wasn't. It was a ritual, masculine and tribalistic. First the apron was flourished, like a bullfighter's cape. The razor was lifted again to catch the flames of light. then laid gently on a fresh towel on the nightstand. My father wet the shaving brush at the filled basin and whipped the soap into a lather. "Now you'll get a shave, son," he said, and he brushed Jay's cheeks with delicate strokes until a snowy beard flowered there. Jay grown old.

My father whistled softly through his teeth. "Now you'll see," he murmured. "A shave." His hands were full of grace as he wielded the razor without disturbing the fluids that dripped into Jay's arm from a bedside stand.

Whole blood now. It had a strange sound. Like whole milk. Pure creamery butter. Wholesome, nourishing.

The razor scraped against Jay's jaw. My father whistled, clucked, almost did a little dance step as he leaned back to survey his work. He patted, wiped, and then the apron was off with a final twirling flourish.

"Bravo!" I said, and rushed to put my face against Jay's.

"Ah," he said. "Thanks, Mr. B. That feels wonderful."

35

I called the floor nurse and asked if Martin had any
visitors. She said that his parents had just left.

He was in a room with three beds. There was a boy of
his own age in one, asleep, while the television set
mounted on the wall above him played soundlessly. It was
a Biblical movie and great throngs raged silently across
the Sinai Desert. The other bed was unoccupied and
Martin was sitting in a chair next to his. "Martin," I said.
"Jay wants you to have this." I put the camera on the bed.

"Oh Sandy," he said. "How is he?"

I shrugged, unable to meet his eyes.

"Isn't there *anything* . . . ?"

"No."

I looked at him. He was getting well, gaining weight
and losing that ethereal delicacy. He seemed less vulnerable to me.

"I was lucky to be with Jay," he said. "I don't just mean
because of the photography or because we were friends.

This is crazy—but sometimes when the days were slow, I would just lie there and daydream and stuff. I would pretend that Jay was my father." He looked down and gave a quick laugh that was more like a hiccup. "And that you were my mother. Crazy. I told you."

So we had common dreams. "Not so crazy."

"Well, I used to feel bad at night, when I would think about it. I would try to get back into the dream, you know, pretending that Jay and I were in a tent somewhere camping out or at the beach. I felt as if I was disloyal to my mother and father. They're really *good,*" he said.

"I know that, Martin."

"No, it's not that. I mean, they can't help being themselves. I *know* it, but there are times when I get angry with my father because of his voice. It's not his fault, he can't help it, but I feel like yelling at him to clear his throat or shut up or something. I wish that my mother was different, that she wouldn't look at me like she's trying to save me or *eat* me up. Even before I was sick. Then I feel lousy, because they seem so sad, like a pair of old babies. I feel *older* than them."

"Martin, that's nothing new. We all become older than our parents, eventually. It's a natural process. You just came to it a little early. It's as if you're up in some high place where you can see everything, their whole history, their future. I think that I know more than my parents, that I could solve their problems and their mysteries if I only had the chance." As I said it, I realized that it was true, that I believed it.

"With you and Jay," he said, "it was only fun."

"That's because you were pretending."

"I really love my parents," Martin said doubtfully.

"I know you do."

He reached out and touched the camera. "Thanks."

"When are you going home?" I asked.

"Soon. In a week or so. I feel funny because I can hardly remember what it was like outside this place. I mean I can remember but I can hardly concentrate on how it *felt*, to go to school, to sleep in my room, to be with my friends. Now the hospital seems more like real life."

"You'll go right back to things," I told him. Then I thought for a while of last words to say to him. I might ask him to come and see me, to call, to keep in touch. I might ask to see the photographs that he would take with Jay's camera or just to let me know what happens to him.

The boy in the other bed woke then, blinked at the television screen and pushed the remote control button, bringing the roaring chorus of the throng to life.

I saw that Martin was turned inward, arranging his thoughts into words. Then, before he could say anything, I gave him a violent hug and went out of the room.

He was standing next to my car when I came out of the hospital. I wondered how long he had been standing there. What did he want?

"I saw your car," he said in greeting. It was very cold and he moved around in little dancing steps like a boxer, his hands in his pockets.

"So I see."

"I wondered how you were."

"Is your friend still here? In the hospital?"

"Who?—oh, Pete. No, he went home a couple of weeks ago. He's even been to the office a few times."

I blew vapor from my mouth like dragon fire. "Then why did you come here?"

He looked genuinely hurt. His brow furrowed and the

smile left his face in a visible stroke. "I was nearby, in the neighborhood. When I saw the hospital, I thought of you. That's all. I drove in and saw your car."

"Francis," I said. "You have a family, don't you? A wife, and children?" I remembered the baby seat in the front of the station wagon.

"Yes. I have four kids . . ."

I saw them suddenly, in my mind's eye: the four children in sleepers, blond, sturdy, standing in order of size, and his wife, tall and thin, with ruined bleached hair and a worried face. "Then what do you want?"

"I don't *want* anything," he said. "I was thinking of you. I feel sort of responsible for you, the way that you do when you save someone's life."

"You're not responsible for me."

"Oh, I don't mean it literally. Let's say that I felt, that I *feel* something for you because of what's happening. I've appointed myself a sort of guardian angel to you." He laughed, and in the cold lamplight I noted the perfection of his teeth, the prominent thrust of his jaw.

"St. Francis," I said, and was sorry when he blushed a deep color. "I'm sorry. Forgive me."

"It's my own fault, I guess," he said. "Maybe it does seem strange, but you were the loneliest-looking . . ."

I patted his arm. It was startlingly solid. "Francis, I am sorry. You get sort of paranoid after a while. You question everybody's motives, even your own. Why do I come here all the time, when he sleeps for hours? Why do I go home? Do I feel enough? Oh God, I'm always having a scene with you in this damn parking lot."

"Let's get out of here," he said, inspired. "Do you want coffee? Or a drink?"

Now I owed him something. And it would be somewhere to go that was not the hospital or home again. "A drink," I said.

"Good. Fine. We'll come back later and get your car."

I thought of what the parking lot would be like then, with the visitors gone and only the few cars of the doctors and night attendants left, as if it were an abandoned stage set.

"No," I said. "I don't want to come back here. I'll follow you."

Out on the street I drove behind him, signaling when he did, turning carefully after him, like an obedient child. We drove for a mile or so, and then Francis' car slowed and he signaled a left turn at the parking lot of a place that called itself Freddy's in blinking blue neon lights. There were a dozen cars or so already parked, and when Francis opened my door, muted sounds of life, music, voices seeped through the walls to us.

We sat at a small table. I didn't take my coat off, although Francis gestured with his hand for it.

We ordered drinks and sat facing one another for an uncomfortable space of time, touching the coasters and matches on the table. I opened and shut my purse several times, peering inside as if I checked on some living creature imprisoned there. At the mirrored bar, people laughed, leaning toward one another in the darkness. Glasses clinked and the music wailed at a distance. What was I doing there after all? Now the question was new. Sitting there like a transient in my overcoat, I wondered what *I* wanted.

"I have three daughters," Francis said. "The baby is a boy."

"That must have made you very happy."

"Oh, he's a terrific kid. All boy. But the girls are great too. I would have settled for all girls."

"I have two boys," I said, trying to remember them.

"But my wife is nervous since the boy. She says the baby makes her nervous, that boys are different."

197

"Well, I guess they are."

"No, not in the way she means. She said that even when he was an infant, just lying there. He made her nervous."

I wondered what he wanted me to say. Something reassuring? Something clinical about postpartum depression?

But he swirled the liquid in his glass and said, "She's a good girl. She tries hard, but sometimes I don't know what she wants."

I smiled what I hoped was an appropriate smile.

"Are you still cold? Shall I take your coat?"

I was warmer by then, but somehow my coat had become a fortress. I shook my head. "I'd rather wear it." I looked at my watch, not really noting the time. "I can't stay too long anyway."

He signaled for the barmaid, but I shook my head again. "Not for me," I said.

"Ah, listen, don't go yet. I haven't even talked to you."

"I know," I said. "But it's getting late." But my husband is dying. But I know what you really want, that fast, desperate fuck in the back of the station wagon, among the domestic litter of your four children. But I think that I am dying too, some moral or spiritual death that defies definition. But I am falling from some unfathomable height forever and ever.

"So then you're going?" he said. "But at least you're not angry. At least we're friends." He put his large hand on the back of my neck, that place that longs for comfort. "I'm glad that you came," he said. He walked with me out to the parking lot, past the bar, where a man said, "Hey don't go yet, blondie, the fun's just starting."

I paid Joseph and sent him home. Then I went into the bedroom and lay down with my arms folded under my head. I could only lie there for a few minutes. I felt a

198

terrible restlessness, as if there were urgent errands I could not remember. I jumped up and went to the window and looked out at the street where snow had been pushed into dreary gray drifts. I walked into the children's room and found Paul uncovered again, the blankets in a mad tangle between his legs. Sleeping, he resisted as I pulled them away. "No," he said in his dream.

"It's all right," I whispered, putting the blankets around his shoulders. He flung them off again with one violent gesture. In the other bed Harry was wrapped and curled like some hibernating creature. His mouth was open, as if in surprise.

I went into the kitchen then and began to open cupboards and drawers and slam them shut again. I opened the refrigerator and put my face into the cold air. I looked at the double row of eggs, the bright containers of milk. In the back, on the top shelf, I found half of a lemon, blue-furred, its rind curling inward. I carried it, holding it away from me as if it were something dangerous, and put it on the counter. God, what else was in there?

Methodically, I took everything out, found forgotten cheese, a dried half-sandwich from Harry's lunch, a green lollipop welded to the shelf. It was true—for the past weeks I had noticed nothing, feeling weak and convalescent each morning. Sometimes I didn't make the beds or clear the breakfast dishes. Even rising and dressing myself was a triumph over apathy.

I filled a basin with warm water and ammonia and began to wash the inside of the refrigerator. The fumes burned my nostrils and made me cough, but I inhaled them as if they were the fumes of some marvelous hallucinatory drug, designed to cancel memory and longing. I scrubbed, reaching into corners, scraping sticky patches off with my fingernails. When I was finished with the refrigerator, I went out into the hall and dumped the rotting food down the incinerator. Then I came back in again and lit the oven light. Grease had baked into a hard dark crust on the walls of the oven. Using steel wool, I scraped and rubbed until they were shining and my fingertips were raw. Ah, just look inside here, Gretel, and help me to light the fire. Hee hee hee my old eyes can't see . . .

I took a rag and a can of polish and attacked the furniture in the living room until the rag was damp and black. Then I went into the bathroom and washed the tile and scrubbed the toilet and the floor of the stall shower, where thin slabs of soap had melted into thick cream. On my hands and knees, I washed the bathroom floor, seeking matted clumps of hair in the corners. Gotcha! I was breathless by then, and flushed, but I felt strangely excited and I went through the apartment looking everywhere, stalking dirt with a wild eye—polishing, scrubbing, wiping—take that! And that! And that!—as if this were my true enemy being vanquished at last.

Later I sat in the living room, panting, my hair falling forward over my eyes and I thought, now what? Now what? Now what? My fingers thrummed on the arm of the chair.

Then the doorbell rang and when I looked through the peephole, Mr. Caspar's sad brown eye looked back at me. I opened the door and saw that he was carrying a cake, still hot, its fragrance rising in steam from the pan. He looked at me quizzically, and I brushed my hair back with my hand. It stank from ammonia and chlorine. I tried to tuck the tail ends of my shirt into my skirt and then I gave up, my hands making jerky gestures. "Well, come in. Is that for us? It's lovely."

He set the cake on the kitchen counter and sniffed at the air.

"Oh," I said. "Just tidying things up. Everything was a mess. It's the ammonia. My hands smell, they look like prunes." I held them out and then quickly withdrew them and put them behind my back. I laughed. "I probably have housemaid's knee, too."

Mr. Caspar smiled. "I thought about you all day and then I baked that." He nodded toward the cake.

"Let's eat it then!" I said, suddenly hungry, ravenous.

"Maybe it's too hot . . ." he said, but I began to put dishes and coffee mugs on the table with a nervous clatter, thinking he'll think I'm mad. Then I ate three pieces of cake, greedily, even licking my fingers after the last slice.

"Oh," I said, shutting my eyes. "Heavenly. Marvelous."

"Then you're all right? I thought . . ."

I took a deep breath. "Yes, yes," a sense of peace and order returning. "Just a little crazy. You're a quieting influence, you know."

"Me?" He stood up and began to collect the dishes from the table and put them into the sink. He swept crumbs up neatly with his hand and wrapped the rest of the cake in foil.

I leaned against the table, watching him with my chin resting on my folded arms. "Is she gone again?" I asked.

He nodded. "And I will have to listen for the weather report. Someone in the elevator today said maybe heavy snow again tonight."

"Again and again and again."

"What we need are green things. Spring."

"To restore hope and destroy memory. Ah, you're a romantic, Mr. C." I took a towel and began to dry a cup.

"Her real name is Edith, you know," he said. "She was eighteen years old when we married and I couldn't convince her of her beauty. 'Am I?' she asked. 'Am I?' "

I put the radio on, listening for the weather report.

"Jay was going to do a wonderful essay on life in the city. Someday I'll show you his photographs."

"The things that happen to us aren't fair," he said.

"Today, I said good-bye to Martin. He'll be going home soon."

"That boy in the hospital?"

"Yes."

Mr. Caspar went to the kitchen window. "If the weather would only be warmer . . ." His words trailed off. On the radio a dance band of the forties played a forgotten ballad. He turned around, and thinking of nothing, I walked toward him and held my arms out. To embrace? To be embraced? His hand circled my waist and he began to lead me into a dance, a slow, dated fox-trot. My forehead rested against his cheek, and I shut my eyes, my feet remembering the music for me, and the rhythm. We danced closely and I put both arms around him. I could feel his heart flutter against me. Out of the kitchen then, slowly, slowly, and into the hallway, where the music became faint, and our feet were silent on the carpet. We turned into the bedroom, where a small bedside lamp was lit. Then the music was too distant, and we only stood together, rocking gently.

I looked at his face, clasping it between my hands. The mask-smile was gone at last. He turned my palm up to his mouth and kissed it. "Yes," I said, and together we opened his shirt. Then I sat down and pulled my shirt open as well, while he watched with this new face, intense, waiting. As he undressed, I watched him too. I had never seen a man of his age without any clothes before and I saw that he was like a detailed drawing for an anatomy class, a drawing that stresses frayed muscle and sharply drawn blue veins and bony structure. I took his hand and curved it to my breast. Then I looked at him and saw that an erection had risen from the ruins. Magic, magic man.

He said my name in a hoarse whisper and then his hand moved, wandering down, down into darkness. "Leonard," he whispered, giving me his name to make intimacy seem reasonable and decent.

Here I go, I thought, and my hand found him and he grew out of grasp. With a last fleeting thought of, oh, *this bed,* I lay back and drew him in.

Later, when I woke, the room was in half-light. I woke him too, so that he would be gone before the children were up. Done and done and done.

36

Jay slept so much that I became used to it, to the long bedside vigils where I would sit drooped in thought, or nonthought, suffering instant lapses of memory. What day was it? What time? What had I been thinking only a few minutes before?

But then there were times when he came sharply and suddenly awake, emerging from one of those long and enervating dreams. He would continue conversations begun in the dream, fix me with his eyes, and demand a response. He was there again, but he was not quite himself. Drugged, drained, pummeled into hopelessness. It scared me because I never knew what to expect, and I was ashamed, because this was the only contact possible, the only thing left between us, and I wanted to avoid it.

"The policies," he began one day while his eyes were still closed.

I was startled out of my slouch. "Sweetheart," I said.

"We talked about that. Don't you remember? I spoke to Murray. We took care of everything."

"Yeah," he said. "It comes back. Do they call?"

"Who?"

"I don't know. Everybody. The crew. Murray. Jerry."

"Yes yes, they all do." Sick with guilt, I knew that I wanted him to sleep again. He had interrupted that strange new state of nothingness I had been clever enough to discover, and he was leading me back to reality. If we talked anymore it would become painful, real, catastrophic. "Do you want some water, darling?" That was a safe topic —the diminishing needs of a diminishing man.

But he didn't even bother to answer. "There are things you have to do, Sandy," he said.

"What things?"

"Take care of some of my stuff. You could sell some of the equipment, the cameras."

"I gave the Rolleiflex to Martin. You told me," I said, worried that he had forgotten and would feel betrayed.

But he only nodded, shutting his eyes again.

Just sleep, I thought. Sweet nothing sleep. I could do it myself right now if there was some place to lie down.

"I keep thinking about the book," Jay said.

The book! I felt an instant throb of jealousy. Why did he think about that? Why didn't he think about the children, about me? But I recognized my own lack of fairness and reason. After all the book was an extension of himself. When he was gone the book would be the real and final proof of himself. As far back as I could remember it was the thing he most looked forward to. Not to its completion, perhaps, but to its growth, to the very act of doing it.

"I wish I could have finished it," he said, and he might have been talking about anything, even his own life.

"I know," I said.

"I took my own sweet time."

"There's a lot there," I said. "You did a lot."

He sighed. "Would you look through it for me, Sandy? Would you see if you can get it into any order, make some sense of it?"

"Sure," I said. "I can do that. I have anyway. I do."

"What?"

"Look through it sometimes when I go home." I felt shy, embarrassed, as if I had been discovered in some naive and romantic practice.

"Maybe you can show it to somebody someday," he said.

"You mean try and get it published, Jay? Is that what you mean?"

"I don't know."

"That's a *good* idea," I said, trying to force some excitement into the monotone of my voice. "It's a beautiful book, Jay. I'm going to do it this week. Look through the folder, get things going for you."

"It wouldn't have much of a chance," he said. "It needs work."

"Who knows? Listen, what do you want to call it? Something simple and right to the point, I think. New York, a Photographic Essay. Or New York City, A Life Story. Is that corny? What do you think?"

"I don't know." He turned his head away, as if he were bored, weary of the subject.

But I felt compelled to continue, desperately chatty, like a woman being eased out of a love affair. I said positive things, things that implied the future. What was wrong with me? I couldn't stop.

"Ah, who gives a damn," he said then, into the wall. "Who gives a fucking damn about anything."

And I found myself sinking back into the chair, the new

false energy instantly spent. He was right. Who gives a damn. Who cares. "Darling," I said. "Do you think you can sleep? Will you try to sleep?"

His voice came with a muffled resonance, his face still turned away. "I'm not tired," he said, and fell instantly asleep.

37

In the small solarium at the end of the corridor, relatives and friends of the terminal patients retreated during
the day and night when they were relieved of their death-
watch. After a few days, faces became familiar, and particular habits, expected. A woman in a gray coat never
removed it, as if she were incurably cold in that over-
heated room, or as if she would be called any moment for
an urgent errand outdoors. She indulged in a series of tics
in compulsive order. First she would crack her knuckles
one at a time, the left hand first, always. Then she would
stretch, turning her head from side to side, releasing more
crackling sounds into that silence. Then finally, she would
clear her throat with a noise so desperate that everyone
would look up at once. For days she spoke to no one,
tented in her overcoat, while her husband, who had been
an orthodontist somewhere in Queens, died of cancer.

Another woman was more verbal. Her mother was dying
of what seemed to be all the complications of old age.

The daughter took her seat in the solarium with an introductory sigh that invited conversation. Her hair was always set in rollers and clips, only slightly obscured by a green print scarf. She brought food with her in tiny brown bags, and when she was not speaking she rattled and rummaged inside the bags for her sandwiches and cookies. "Would you like one?" she always asked. "Would *you* like one? Would you? It's tuna."

After two days the woman in the gray coat would not even answer her and the woman in the curlers drew up one side of her mouth in a significant expression.

Two men, obviously brothers, sometimes held hands while they waited news of their father. Their wives, who visited only occasionally, didn't like one another, and spoke in affected voices.

The first week after Jay had been brought to that floor, an old man died in the room across from his. His children decided at the last minute to bring their senile mother from a nursing home nearby, so that the parents might see each other one more time. But by the time they arrived, the old man had already entered a coma and could not respond to anyone. The old woman came out of the elevator and made a great deal of noise. Perhaps she was deaf, or excited, or simply frightened. But her voice seemed to pierce the brain. "What's the matter, *now?*" she shrieked. "Oh, my legs!" The middle-aged children, each supporting her under one arm, looked at each other doubtfully. But they couldn't retreat now. They were *there*. The old couple were within a few feet of each other. Their mother and their father.

"Mama!" the old woman shouted. "They drag me on these feet!"

A nurse rushed from her station, saying, "Shhhh, you'll have to keep her quiet."

The old woman looked at her fiercely, her chin trembling, but she was still for a few minutes. When they came to the father's room, she shrugged off the supporting hands of her children and walked to the bedside. The old man was propped on his bed, almost sitting, the center of some strange universe where all tubes led to him and entered him everywhere. He was the color of dying old men, and he made rasping noises deep in his throat, that noise of failing machines. Before she could be stopped, the old woman grasped him by the front of his nightgown, half pulling him up from the bed, so that his long white hair fell back in pale threads. "Morris!" she yelled. "Pull yourself together!"

By the time the children reached her, she had dislodged the tubes from his nostrils and knocked his head a few times against the bars of the headboard. "Mama!" They looked at each other accusingly. The reunion had not been such a good idea after all. She didn't know how to say a proper good-bye.

As the elevator door opened, she said, "Morris, I'm walking on fire!" and was heard from no more. The husband lived two more days.

Jay, I thought, pull yourself together. Enough, enough. He woke, asked, "It is Monday?" Slept.

Who says a proper good-bye after all? How? To his eyes, to his tender sac, to his white feet, to his hands.

The nurses came to do things, mysterious rituals of sheet-changing and sponging. Down the hall again to the solarium. The woman in curlers ate a meat loaf sandwich, picking crumbs off her skirt with fastidious fingers, and dropping them back into the brown bag. The odor was the odor of school cafeterias, the sound of her chewing the only thing to be heard anywhere.

Izzy came in her moleskin coat, brought little wrapped

mints, a pocket pack of Kleenex, change for the telephone. When my throat became too dry, or thick with sorrow, I would suck one of the mints, sometimes forgetting and splintering it with my teeth. Then all day when I sighed or drew deep breaths, I felt a winter wind rush in and burn the back of my throat.

The two brothers came in, nodded at me, at Izzy, and took their places. The woman with the curlers ate Yankee Doodles. She licked the white cream from the wrappers.

Izzy put her arm through mine. "Who's with your kids?" I asked.

"Eddie," she said.

I raised my eyebrows. It was Saturday.

"He's their *father,* you know. He's taking them to the Aquarium. Ah," she said, looking around her, inhaling the atmosphere, "how can you stand it?"

I opened one of the mints and put it into my mouth. "I can't." Tears came to my eyes.

"Oh Sandy." She pulled at her fingers as if they might come off.

The two brothers stood up and went out toward their father's room.

Izzy leaned closer and touched my shoulder. "Sandy, listen," she said, in an urgent whisper. "Do you know about Eddie and me?"

I shook my head.

"Well, sometimes he stays."

I stared at her and the melting mint slid down my throat.

"For part of the night, I mean."

I couldn't think of anything to say, but she was afraid that I hadn't understood. "You know, I still sleep with him. Once in a while."

"Izzy," I said. "This isn't a church."

"I know. I just wanted to tell someone. I'll bet you think I'm a damn fool. Or worse."

I shook my head again.

"Oh, what's the difference?" she asked. "You look around here and you realize it doesn't matter what you do. Or if you last long enough, it won't matter." She looked at me anxiously, and I realized that she was waiting for some word of comfort or approval.

"Of course," I said.

The woman in curlers came over and offered something from her bag. "My mother has a heart of iron," she said, and I knew with a terrible certainty when she would comb her hair out.

38

My night ritual wouldn't work anymore. It was strange and frightening, as if there can be an expiration date on experience. Or maybe it was all in the natural order of things. Jay was dying and so was everything that had existed between us.

Sleep should be easier, I thought, as simple as all the other body functions. But it wasn't. I used to sleep quickly and well after lovemaking. Then talk was an effort, a valiant attempt at continued companionship. Our heads were as heavy as those of children kept up past their bedtime.

Jay was the bearer of water and oranges, the one to check windows and door locks. I'd watch him in his rounds through half-lidded eyes, feeling thirsty, and sleepy, and warm. I lay across the bed, into his territory, still looking for warm places his body had left. Still trying to fit us together, our shadows and our thoughts. Jay came back to bed bearing two brimming glasses of water, an absurd and naked waiter. His hair even darker with dampness, his chest hair flattened, his penis still half-erect, as if in fond memory. "You have a lovely, lovely body," I once said.

"We aim to please, missus," he answered and the water sloshed over the sides of the glasses. I could hardly stay awake long enough to drink it. Ah, sweet and natural sleep.

I tried to bring that back now, tried to conjure up the past again, willing to take whatever came along, the good moments or the bad. But nothing came at all. There is no life after death, I was convinced of that. But the life before it should be a more tangible and solid thing.

I kept the light on in the room the way I did when I was a child, but now it was a seduction. I *wanted* ghosts to enter. When I slept finally I always came awake abruptly, as if someone shook me, and then it was to that strange mixture of natural and artificial light. I tried to bring back the lovemaking, or the quarrels, or even ordinary domestic moments, but nothing held. There were other people awake in the building. Lumber creaked, plumbing complained, and the real world intruded. Maybe I had outgrown the need for sleep. There was a hot dry energy I had never known before. But I couldn't apply it to anything. Books refused to be read, food became inedible, and simple television programs couldn't be followed, as if language itself had become obsolete. I walked back and forth in the bedroom saying, I have to think, I have to think.

I opened the drawer of the night table. Next to my diaphragm, to old check stubs and some loose pennies, was the vial of sleeping capsules. I took one and held it up to the bed lamp, trying to see through it. But its redness was as dense and mysterious as sleep itself. I could just take it and be done with it. It would be like a swift and painless blow to the head. But I hesitated. It would be the end of something that I dreaded to give up. The end of my control over things, that was one part. The end of memory as fantasy, of Jay entering this room through the magic of my will. His voice and his presence. It was a leave-taking in a way, a rehearsal for the real thing. Good-bye. Good-bye then, I thought, weary and sick with the knowledge.

I put the capsule on the back of my tongue and forced it down my throat without water.: I gagged slightly and then it was gone. I climbed back into bed again, half sitting against both pillows, waiting for its journey and mine to begin.

39

"Sandy?"

"I'm here."

"Sandy?"

"I'm here, Jay, I'm right here."

"Okay. I was dreaming." He smiles, sleeps, frowns. Dogs bark, phones ring. "If it's for me . . ."

"Shhhh. It's nothing."

In the dream he drives a car, hands up to steer, foot braced against the sheet. He stops short, bed creaks.

"Don't, Jay. It's nothing." Not wanting to touch him now. Those greenstick bones. What can we do to put flesh on those bones? Dem bones.

"Who's there? Who came in?"

"No one. It's only me." The machinery of my brain. The hurricane of my breath.

"I keep dreaming."

"I know."

"Did the baby cry?"

"No. It was in your dream."

The good nurse comes, leans over with her cloud of dark hair, mother hair. Brings a cup of tea. The cup rattles in the saucer.

I carry it out to the solarium, where daylight is dazzling. Why do we die in dark places?

The woman in the gray coat is inconsolable. "I am inconsolable," she says, and cracks her knuckles. The report is as sharp as the noise from a fired gun.

My mother comes on tiptoe, her shoes squeaking. She grimaces in agony at their noise. "Lie down, tootsie."

"I can't. Lying down, I sink, I drown."

The woman in the gray coat stretches and sighs. The sound is deafening.

We walk back to the room. Thundering hooves.

Jay is lying on his side with his back to the door. His hospital gown is loosely closed and the bones of his spine are like carefully placed white stones in a path. "Sandy?"

"I'm here, darling."

Blood comes from Jay in an endless ribbon.

The bad nurse enters and stops it with the fierceness of her ability. Bad triumphs over evil.

I am inconsolable.

"Sandy?"

40

I walked down the hall toward the telephone booths. A black orderly moved, whistling, past me. He was wheeling a garbage cart. I reached into my purse and found a coin to call the operator. "Operator," I said. "I want to make a person-to-person call to Honolulu, Hawaii." My voice was clear and steady and reasonable. I told her to charge the call to my home telephone number. I even gave her Jay's name and the address of our apartment.

Then I listened to a cacophony of sounds: bells, whistles, clicks, hums. Operators spoke to one another and their words were scattered, as if spoken in a strong wind. Outside the telephone booth, a man waited to make a call. He looked at his watch, he rubbed his nose, and looked at his watch again. Voices said numbers and names. They thanked one another.

The man began to pick his nose. On the wall above the telephone someone had written, Call Erica if you want it. This is an underwater call, I thought. Cables coiled like serpents on the floor of the ocean. Call Erica if you want it. The man outside did a nervous little soft-shoe step. There was no air in the telephone booth. The telephone booth was under water.

Then Mona said, "Hello? Hello?"

What time is it in Honolulu? What will I do when the water is over my head?

"New York?" Mona was incredulous. "Sam, Sam, hurry up, it's the children!"

Then my voice began to speak, shattering sea life for miles and miles.

41

He died in his sleep, in my sleep, as I nodded, dozing in the waiting room. My shoes were off and my skirt twisted around so that the zipper was in the front. The nurse woke me, called my name. I could not, would not remember where I was. I chose to be dreaming or back in childhood, wakened by my mother for school, or anywhere that was not here. "No," I said, sealing out the invasion of light with my heavy eyelids. I shoved against her, pushing away the reality of her presence, her inevitable news. Oh, I wanted to sleep, sleep.

They woke me after Harry was born. I had gone out in that last moment of creation. "It's a boy! Look Sandy, it's a boy. He's fine. It's all over." I came awake to astonishment and pleasure. Jay, inflated with joy, my mother and father, transformed into grandparents. Plants, flowers, greeting cards that celebrated life.

"I won't," I said to this nurse, but she would not allow it. Her urging became less gentle and I had to open my eyes. The two brothers were there, huddled together in a corner, and the woman in the gray coat was asleep in her chair. Wake *her,* I thought. Let it be *their* news. Why did she pick on me?

I sat up and rubbed my eyes. The nurse sat next to me on the couch and she took my hand. "He's gone," she said. "In his sleep."

Gone. But she meant dead. Gone was someone gone from a room, someone escaped from a prison. Dead was no breath, no pain, no pleasure. It was nothing.

"Do you want something?" she asked. "A sedative?"

But I shook my head. I had been asleep, sedated when Harry was born, so that I would not feel the final and earthshaking thrust of his head. "Give me something. Hurry up!" I had ordered. Who wanted to be a martyr to the birth of a stranger? The mask came and I rose to meet it, grateful and greedy.

But now it was necessary to be alert, to know everything. The others in the room stared at me, their eyes like the watchful eyes of small animals in a forest.

"Did he say anything?" I asked the nurse, thinking of an urgent message, last words that would unravel the mystery.

But she said, "No, quietly, in his sleep. I was with him."

Not me, ear cocked for final sounds, but this strange and gentle woman, who was there because it was her job. At the end of the week she would get a paycheck, with deductions, for sitting with my husband while he died. It was the strangest thing to think about, as if I were trying to understand the mores of another culture.

"Would you like to see him?" she asked, and I drew away from her for a moment. Of course not. Of course I didn't want to see him. All the terrible death words rushed into my head. Corpse, body, remains. God. But I had promised myself that I would know everything. The ritual would be completed. I stood, light-headed and uncertain. The tiled floor was cold under my stockinged feet, and she led me, holding my elbow, like a mother leading a child to the bathroom during the night.

The room had been emptied of all the paraphernelia: the tubes, trays, the machines that defied this terrible and natural process of life. I hoped for a moment that he would appear to be sleeping, that I could be comforted by all the American phrases of solace. He is just away. He is only asleep. He is out of it now. At least his suffering is over. See how peaceful he looks.

But he didn't even look like Jay anymore. It was the right room. There was the yellow water stain under the windowsill, the familiar whorls in the wood of the door. And there on the bed was a dead body, nothing more. The nurse was right. Gone was the right word after all. The force of life, gone. The miracle of emotion, gone. Nothing.

I left the room, padding silently down the hall to get my shoes and coat. I wanted to go home and get on with the real business of mourning. But it wouldn't wait. The others in the waiting room made the first ovations. "Sorry. Out of pain now. At peace. So sorry." They murmured, fluttered and flapped near me until tears burned in my throat. Don't, I warned myself. What did those stock phrases have to do with Jay, with me, with our real lives? I would not let them enter me and take hold. And yet the texture of that gray coat against my skin, the whispering chorus of their voices, the real and human smell and warmth of their breath invaded me and I passed among them weeping.

I went home and I let myself into the apartment, going quickly past the dumb, expectant faces of my parents and the children. I went into the bedroom and I shut the door. They called timidly. "Sandy? Are you all right? Sandy?" They knocked on the door. But I would not answer. I lay down on the bed, the only place where it was possible to begin.